Yorkshire Mysteries

Book One:
The Pilfered Pouch

Dianne LeMay

For Mom and Dad, with love and gratitude.

All Rights Reserved
Two Penny Publishing

ISBN: 0615634311
ISBN-13: 978-0615634319

York, England

October 1468

Chapter One

Bess Cardwell moved her knight in front of her brother's bishop in order to block his next move. He tried to keep from smiling when he then captured her queen.

"That is not fair, Will!" she exclaimed, stomping her foot for emphasis.

"It is only unfair because you are losing, little sister," he said playfully.

They were sitting in the solar of Cardwell Hall, a fire blazing in the hearth, munching on roasted chestnuts. They would normally have been playing their favorite game of chess at Cardwell Manor, their country home several miles outside the city walls of

York, but their father was required to be in town to settle a few pressing business matters and it appeared the family would be here for quite a while. Bess had garnered a promise from him that they would be back in the Manor for Christmas, but she knew first-hand her father did not always keep his promises.

"I believe it is time to put Margaret to bed," Alice Cardwell announced. She had been lounging on the settle, where two-year old Margaret had fallen fast asleep on her mother's lap.

Bess didn't bother to look up from the chess board, however William managed a light-hearted, "Goodnight, Mother."

After Alice and Margaret had left the room, Bess glared at William and hissed, "How can you call that woman 'Mother'? She is not our mother, and you well know it!"

William did know it, but preferred to do whatever he could to keep the peace in his torn household. "She is not the enemy. If she likes that I call her mother, so be it. I do not see why you cannot come to terms with father's new wife. It is not as though you can remember our own mother."

"I cannot. But you can, Will, and that is why your indiscretion is unforgivable!"

With that outburst, Bess ran from the room. She was in such a hurry to get to her bedchamber that she bumped into her father as he was escorting a fellow wool merchant from his antechamber.

"You must not run in the house, Bess. What our guest must think of a girl of sixteen who is so unruly, I cannot imagine," Sir James scolded.

"Nonsense!" Sir Charles Heatherton was quick to come to Bess' aid. "My own daughter still runs about like a wild banshee, and she is but two weeks from her sixteenth birthday." He looked down at her. "You will come to Jane's birthday feast, will you not, my dear?"

"Yes Sir Charles, thank you," Bess responded shyly, too mortified to look at her own father for fear of the disapproval she might find upon his face. Instead she fastened her gaze upon Sir Charles. He was a heavy-set man, much her father's age, with a ruddy complexion and bright blue eyes. She noticed the intricately carved golden clasp that held his deep purple cloak about his shoulders, took in his expensively trimmed midnight blue doublet and his shiny black riding boots.

"Now run along Bess," her father told her.

"Yes sir. Goodnight," she said as she proceeded to walk slowly down the hallway to her chamber.

Once inside, she threw herself upon her bed, pulled the coverlets up over her head and began to sob gently. She knew her actions had been childish; knew, too, that her crying now was further evidence that she was not as grown up as she thought herself to be.

William had been right; she couldn't remember their mother. She was only three when her mother had died, but even so, she couldn't help feeling ashamed that she didn't have at least one memory. She used to lie awake at night, straining her mind to recall a moment, a smell, a touch, but it was always to no avail. When her father had married Alice, she tried even harder, but found the past to be long forgotten. Now, as Bess wiped her tears, she wondered if her father had forgotten, too.

"Ouch!" Jasmine exclaimed as she wiped the blood from her pricked finger.

She was attempting to complete her latest piece of needlework, but was having difficulty focusing on what she was doing. As she sat in the second-storey window seat of the house she shared with her father, her mind wandered as she looked down onto the street below. The sight was as familiar to her as the back of her own hand, for she had lived here for all of her sixteen years. Fifteen of those years had been spent in complete happiness with her father and mother, learning at her mother's knee the craft of sewing and embroidery, which provided an extra income for the family.

Her father was a butcher, which was why they lived on the street in York known as The Shambles. He had once told her that the word 'Shambles' was derived from the Anglo-Saxon word 'Shamel', meaning stall or bench, and it was on these benches that the butchers of ancient York had sold their meat.

Even now, all of the men who lived on this street were butchers, and as Jasmine looked below, she could see them in their stalls, with their big knives, cutting the meat of cows and pigs and selling them to the customers strolling along the crowded, narrow street that she called home.

This was not the reason for her distraction, however, and she quickly put away her needlework, knowing that she would not get any work done today. She went to her coffer-chest and pulled out the sack into which she had already placed another gown quite like the one she was currently wearing. She went down the narrow staircase and out the front door, hoping to escape her father's notice.

"Jasmine my dear, where are you off to?" John Bowles' voice was as full-bodied as he was himself, and Jasmine could not simply pretend that she did not hear his question.

"I think you know, Papa," she said, without looking at him, and ran down the street in the direction of the churchyard, the sack she had prepared slung over her shoulder.

Mr. Bowles looked after his daughter and sighed. The next week would be so hard for her, so hard for them both.

Jasmine didn't go to the churchyard, however. Instead she went to the marketplace and found her friends Harry and Tom perusing the stalls, waiting for a vendor to turn his back so they could steal the odd apple or fig.

Jasmine didn't approve of this thievery, however, and slapped Harry in the back of the head when she caught up to him. "You should know better, Harry. You'll get put in the gaol if you're not careful!"

"Aye, I'm always careful, but better than that, I'm lucky too!" Harry's green eyes sparkled with mischief.

They continued down the street in search of their friends, who were soon found and gathered around Jasmine, eyeing each other expectantly. She slowly opened her sack, reached underneath her gown and pulled out the all-important football. Harry quickly grabbed it and the two teams split up and began the game, kicking the ball through the narrow street.

The football was made of a leather-covered pig's bladder filled with dried peas, and Jasmine had the distinction of being its 'keeper' for her team. Luckily, her father had not discovered this or she would be in a great amount of trouble. He often warned her of the dangers of playing football in the crowded streets and forbade her ever to play. But even though she knew that she risked her father's wrath, she continued to play on, needing the freedom and release, the expenditure of energy. Sitting in her house sewing all day did nothing to ease the sadness and frustration she felt. Now, as she raced down the street, she could forget the pain she found so hard to tolerate during the normal course of her day.

Bess fastened her cloak about her shoulders and hurried down the stairs. Her brother William was already outside, waiting for her to begin their weekly excursion to the marketplace. She was just about to pull the latch on the heavy oaken door when she heard Alice calling from behind her.

"Elizabeth, there you are. I have been looking for you," she said as Bess turned to face her.

Everyone in the Cardwell family called her Bess except for her father's new wife, who always referred to her by her given name of Elizabeth. Alice had never asked if she could call her anything else, and Bess had certainly never offered.

"William is waiting for me, and..."

"Let him wait," she said harshly. "I have need of you."

"What do you require, Madame?" Bess asked coldly.

"Margaret's favorite blanket is missing. Have you seen it?"

Bess' face flushed with anger. "If you are accusing me of taking it, you are mistaken."

"I am doing no such thing. I merely wish to know if you remember having seen it. Margaret could hardly sleep last night without its comfort."

Bess wanted to remind Alice that since her bedchamber was next to the little girl's, she need not tell her that Margaret could not sleep, her constant crying had been evidence enough of that fact.

"I have not seen it," she replied, and shut the door behind her with as much force as she could muster.

William had trouble keeping up with Bess as they made their way to the marketplace, and remarked to her that they could take their time, the stalls were not going to up and move before they arrived. He knew that she must have had words with their stepmother; no one riled Bess the way that Alice did.

"She makes me so wroth, Will. Do you know what she accused me of?"

"No dearest. What?"

"She actually accused me of taking little Margaret's blanket!"

"Why would she do that?" he asked.

"For the simple reason that it is missing."

William squeezed his sister's hand. She had taken their father's marriage to Alice much harder than he had. It had taken place a full three years ago, and still Bess had not made her peace with their stepmother. He supposed that Bess was jealous. Having been the only girl in their lives for so long, it would naturally be difficult for her to accept a new woman in her father's life, and when Margaret came just a year later, things seemed to have gotten worse. Their father doted on his new little daughter and William always noticed the pained look on Bess' face when she saw them together.

They were walking down a street known as Colliergate. Many of the streets of York had been named for the trade that was performed there. Colliergate was where the colliers, or charcoal dealers, sold their wares, Hornpot Lane was where the horn workers pursued their craft, and Spurriergate was the street of the spur-makers. There were many more colorfully-named streets that set York apart from the other towns and villages in England, not to mention the white limestone walls that surrounded the city as a fortification against invaders.

William and Bess rounded the next corner, only to find themselves in the middle of a pack of running youths kicking a rounded ball. Bess had never seen anything like it, but before she could make much sense of what was going on, a large girl, almost a head taller than she was, bumped into her, knocking her down on the ground so forcefully that she torn her gown.

The game came to a sudden halt as William helped Bess up, keeping his arm around her for support. He asked Jasmine if she was hurt, but she shook her head.

Bess fixed her eyes on Jasmine, looked her up and down and said, "What kind of a peasant are you, playing this horrid game with all of these boys?"

"I'm no peasant, and you'll take that back before I knock you down again!" Jasmine answered loudly before she could stop herself. She knew that she was in the wrong, endangering others with their game, and would have apologized had Bess not verbally attacked her by calling her a peasant.

William came between the two girls. "You had better leave now if you know what is good for you," he warned Jasmine and her friends.

Jasmine was about to walk away when Bess commented to her brother, "She is as dark as the infidels father has told us about. Do you think she is one, or is that just dirt smeared on her face?"

At that remark, Jasmine flew into a rage and ran toward Bess, but Harry caught hold of her and threw his arms around her waist, stopping her from making a horrible mistake.

"Don't pay her any heed, Jasmine. Let's go home," Harry said soothingly.

William escorted Bess away at the same moment, yet both girls kept an eye on each other until they were out of sight. It would take longer, however, for the memory to cease to burn in each girl's mind.

Chapter Two

Jasmine was still fuming over what that girl had said to her, calling her an infidel, and when Harry's mother set a cup of tea in front of her she drained it without even thinking of politeness. "Excuse me, Mrs. Stopplewick. I didn't mean to be rude."

"Never you mind, lass. That rough and tumble game you children play is enough to give anyone an unquenchable thirst."

Mrs. Stopplewick was a lively woman, robust and as freckled as Harry. She kept a well-stocked herb garden in the back of their house which provided her with various plants necessary for her special 'elixers,' as she liked to call them. They were made in the form of teas, poultices, or lotions, and she distributed them among the various town-folk who were in need of their healing powers. Mrs. Stopplewick would not put a price on her products, however; she preferred to let her buyers pay in whatever form of compensation they could provide, once even receiving a pig's foot for her services. She never failed to remind her customers that God had provided all the medicines the body requires, if people would only look hard enough for them.

The tea which she had given to Jasmine contained the herb Tansy, known to have general healing properties. Last month she had given her an ointment made with Colewort, to ease her muscle aches and pains, which Jasmine sometimes shared with her father when he became overly sore from his work.

Jasmine liked Mrs. Stopplewick immensely and appreciated the drink, not to mention having a private place to change her gown. She hadn't as yet put on the extra one she had packed in the sack that was currently at her feet, was still too angry to think about anything except that wretched girl and her brother.

"I've been meaning to ask you," Mrs. Stopplewick began, after re-filling Jasmine's cup, "your father doesn't approve of you playing football with the boys, does he?"

Jasmine lowered her eyes.

"I didn't think so," she said quietly. "You'd hardly need to change your clothes before you went home if he did."

Jasmine met her gaze and pleaded, "Please don't tell him, I beg you."

"Well he won't hear it from me, that's for certain," she assured the girl as she got up from the table and put a hand on Jasmine's shoulder. "But he should hear it from you."

There was a long pause as Jasmine tried to think of how to respond. She couldn't promise to tell her father, and yet she knew that that was what Mrs. Stopplewick wanted to hear. Instead she said, "May I change my clothes now?"

"Of course, dearie. You know where my bedchamber is, go right ahead."

Once inside the small chamber, Jasmine hastily pulled out the clean gown and slipped it over her kirtle, banishing the dirty one to the bottom of the sack. Before playing football, she always tied her gown up around her knees so that she could move about more freely, which also prevented her from tearing the hem of her garment. She thought about the girl she had bumped into today and her torn gown. She recalled it being a beautiful shade of blue, and thought that it must be worth more than all three of her gowns put together. She had been sorry to see that it was ripped, until the girl had called her a peasant and then an infidel.

The truth was that Jasmine's skin had always been a darker shade than most people's, causing her to feel very self-conscious. Each year she dreaded the coming of summer because the hot sun made her skin a deep brown color and she could do nothing to stop it. Her hair was dark, too, like her eyes, and it was impossibly curly, making it look unkempt at all times. For the most part, she tried not to dwell on her appearance, but occasionally she gave in and felt sorry for herself; this was one of those times.

She thanked Mrs. Stopplewick, said goodbye to Harry, who was busy playing draughts with his little brother, and started to walk home. Her path led her across Holy Trinity churchyard. She made her way through the familiar grave stones until she came to rest at one grave in particular. She knelt down and began to cry, "Mama, why did you have to leave me?"

Alice Cardwell took one look at Bess and exclaimed, "Whatever have you done, Elizabeth? You look positively mussed!"

Bess had tried to cross the great hall without being seen; she had no choice now but to present herself to Alice.

"Some young ruffians were playing a game through the streets today and knocked me down! I am lucky William was with me, or who knows what might have happened!" Bess explained, hoping to exact some sympathy.

"It seems you have come through this ordeal relatively unscathed. See to it that Maude mends and washes your gown immediately, we would not want the stain to settle," Alice responded bluntly.

Bess said nothing, instead went straight to her bedchamber, tore off her soiled gown and did *not* ring for Maude.

Dressed in her undergarments and kirtle, she poured fresh water from the ewer into the richly decorated basin and washed her face and neck, using the expensive scented soap her brother had given her for her birthday. She then threw back the bed hangings and jumped onto the plush mattress made of goose down feathers. Picking up her favorite book, she began to read about the chivalrous Arthur, the beautiful Gwenivere, and the Knights of the Round Table. How she wished she could be among them!

Her thoughts were interrupted by a knock on her door, to which she responded, "Come in," praying to God that it was not Alice who wished to enter.

Instead it was her servant Maude. "Sorry to disturb you, Miss, but Lady Cardwell asked me to see to your torn gown."

"It is there on the floor in front of you, Maude, you may help yourself to it," Bess replied, hoping she would leave immediately.

She did, and Bess was alone again.

Later that day, Bess and William were strolling through the garden, having just eaten a hearty supper of roast pork, boiled mutton, an almond confection, cheese, bread, spiced apples, and wine from Bordeaux.

William patted his stomach as he said, "A good meal, good wine, what more can a fellow ask for?"

"What indeed?" Bess responded absent-mindedly. Twilight was approaching, her favorite time of day, and she breathed in the chilly evening air. She paused by the mulberry tree and asked her brother, "What game were they playing?"

It took a moment for William to comprehend her question, but then answered, "Football."

"They should not be playing it in the streets. It is too dangerous."

"That is true, but remember, they have no courtyard, no field on which to pursue their games like we do," William pointed out.

"I suppose," Bess replied, contemplating this.

"Bess, can I ask you something?" he inquired.

"Certainly."

"Do you feel bad about what you said to that girl?"

"Whatever do you mean? Calling her a peasant?" Bess asked.

"No. I mean when you called her an infidel and said that she was dirty," he ventured, unsure of what his sister's reaction would be.

"Oh that. I have not considered whether I feel bad or not, it is of no consequence to me," she responded plainly.

"But it is of consequence to her," William reminded her.

"You care about the feelings of some unknown town bully who almost killed me?" She knew she was being overly dramatic, but contorted her face in a pout nonetheless.

"Bess, be reasonable. She has feelings just as you do. God loves her just as much as he loves us."

"Please, William, leave God out of this!" She always used his full name when she was less than pleased with her brother.

"I know that you are kind-hearted, Bess. I have seen you give alms to the poor and stop to help complete strangers when they were in need. I have not, however, seen this behavior since Father married Alice. Is it really as bad as that?"

Bess pulled one of the few remaining leaves from the mulberry tree and began to tear pieces from it as she thought of what she could say to her brother to make him understand her feelings.

"Do you remember, four years ago, when I was just twelve and we were having Christmas at the Manor?"

William nodded.

"Father let me sit next to him at the feast, sharing his plate with me and telling me about each of his guests. I felt cherished, Will, like I had never felt before," her face suddenly became clouded, "and like I have never felt since. Surely you can see that everything changed once that woman entered Father's life? Surely you can see that he never has time for me anymore? I do not expect you to understand how I am feeling, since nothing is different between you and Father. You are still his only son. He talks to you of business matters and is seeking to have you educated at Middleham. You have no reason to doubt his love for you. I, however, do!"

William was taken aback by the bluntness of his sister's response and by the raw need he saw in her blue eyes. What could he say to make her feel better? He too, had seen that his father did not seem to be as interested in Bess as he used to be. Should he tell her of his own problems with Father? That he had no desire to go into business or to be educated at Middleham? No, his problems could wait, hers could not. He silently asked God for direction before proceeding cautiously.

"Father still loves you, dearest, I am sure of it. You know that because of him the Guild is becoming increasingly powerful. This means that his responsibilities have also increased. His time is torn between business, the Manor, and his family. He is being pulled in many directions and has not the energy he used to. Besides, being rude to Alice will not endear you to Father, surely you know that?"

Bess nodded, could not look at William as he spoke.

"One thing I do know, Bess, is that God will help you if you will only let Him. Tell Him of your troubles and let Him ease your pain."

"I had no idea you desired a life in the clergy, Will," Bess remarked sarcastically. She threw the remains of the mulberry leaf to the ground and began her slow walk back, trying not to think on her brother's words.

Jasmine poured her father another cup of ale. They had finished their meal of barley bread, cheese, and roasted turnips, and she was now engaged in embroidering a draw-string pouch for Mrs. Stopplewick. The tallow candle on the table beside her was almost burned down to its wick; she would need to light another soon.

"Fancy a game of draughts, my dear?" John Bowles asked.

"Certainly, Papa," she said, knowing her eyes could use the respite from the tedious needlework.

After the board had been set up and the pieces put in place, Mr. Bowles looked at his daughter as she made the first move. He wondered how to bring up the subject they were both focused upon, day and night.

Instead of venturing onto this topic however, he made his counter-move and asked, "You didn't happen to see Harry today, did you?"

"Yes, Papa," was Jasmine's terse response. Did he suspect her of playing football again?

"Tell him to stay out of The Shambles if he's going to practice any more petty thievery. Gives us a bad name, you being such a friend of his."

"I've already told him, Papa. I can't control his actions," she reminded him.

"Aye, but you can control yours. Mr. Thompson the coal dealer told me he heard of a roving football game that was said to include a lass. That couldn't have been you he was referring to, could it?"

Jasmine looked down at the board. "No," she ventured, unsure of whether or not he had any proof of her playing in the game.

"I hope not. The last thing I need is you coming home with a broken bone, or worse yet."

He got up from the table, went to the window and unlatched the shutters, letting the cool night air refresh his lungs. All he could see was blackness except for the dim light of one candle burning in the window of the jettied row house across the street. How could he tell his daughter what he really felt? That not a day passed by when he didn't worry he would lose her just as he had lost his wife, her mother?

Jasmine put the game away in the nearby chest and said, "I'm tired, Papa, I'd like to go to bed."

Mr. Bowles looked into her weary eyes and knew the moment had passed; they would not speak of the unspeakable tonight. "Goodnight, Jasmine."

Once inside her small chamber, Jasmine lay on her bed and tried her best to think of nothing at all.

A week had passed and Bess was busily preparing for another trip to the marketplace, hoping this excursion would be less eventful than the last. She turned her back to Maude, who had been helping her dress for the day, lifted the lid of her coffer-chest and rummaged through it hastily.

"Can I help you find anything, Miss?" Maude asked.

"My pouch seems to be missing. Have you seen it?"

"No, Miss."

Bess' eyes narrowed as she said, "That will be all, Maude. Do not forget to meet me in the courtyard. William cannot accompany me to the marketplace today, so I have need of you."

She had a good idea where her pouch might be, and made her way downstairs to confront Alice with her suspicions. She found her in the solar, playing a game of peek-a-boo with little Margaret.

"Good day, Elizabeth. Would you like to sit here by the hearth with us?" asked Alice, who seemed to be in high spirits this morning.

Bess was put off by her friendly manner, but did not waver in her accusation, saying, "Have you seen my pouch?"

"Yes I have," she surprised Bess by saying. "It is there." She pointed to the window-seat, then added, "Where you left it."

Bess retrieved her pouch, shook it to make sure her coins were still inside, and tied it to her belt. "Thank you. However, I did not leave it there."

"You must be mistaken."

"I assure you I am not," Bess replied sternly and turned to exit the chamber.

"Where are you going, Elizabeth?" Alice asked.

"It is Wednesday, Madame, time for my trip to the marketplace."

"Where is William?"

"He is with Father today."

Alice picked up the baby and rose to her feet. "I do not approve of your going to the marketplace without William."

"I neither asked for your approval, nor do I need it. But if it eases your mind any, Maude will be with me at all times."

"I do not care if Maude or Christ Jesus himself is with you, you are not to leave this house," Alice said icily.

"I do not know if Christ would ever consider a visit to York, Madame, although there are sinners enough. But regardless of who travels with me, I am going."

Bess stormed out of the solar and left the house as quickly as she could. She and Maude hurried through the courtyard and passed the gate, leaving Alice staring at them through the window.

Jasmine took her time on the way back home from Mr. Sowers' shop. She had dropped off a tunic of his that had required mending and had received two pence for her trouble. As she came to the street that would lead her back to The Shambles, she changed her mind and her course and went to the marketplace instead. She decided that she deserved something special today, and thought to buy some apples to make a tart for herself and her father.

She strolled past the stalls and stopped to speak to a few of the vendors she knew, even receiving a commission for a new garment that could earn her a ripe sum. She reached a cart of apples and was perusing the selection, when out of the corner of her eye she spotted the loveliest shade of green she had ever seen. She turned to see what it was, only to be disappointed to find out that the owner of this beautiful green garment was none other than the girl she had bumped into a week ago. The girl was looking at the wares of one of the shopkeepers across the street, and Jasmine could not resist the temptation to follow her. Hidden behind carts of apples, onions, and cabbage, she watched as the girl made her way from shop to shop, unaware of the prying eyes that were upon her.

Jasmine had already taken in her beautiful green gown, noticed now the shimmering silvery-blonde hair, the exquisite porcelain-like skin and dainty features of this young beauty. She was petite, and had a graceful way of walking that made Jasmine feel like an overblown ox. She was now acutely aware of her own plain gown made from inexpensive brown linen and her unruly brown hair atop a head that was beautiful only to her father. She knew the standard of perfection for English women was firmly set; only the blondest of blonde hair, the palest of pale skin, the bluest of blue eyes would do, and all must be found on one slender frame. Jasmine did not meet even one of these requirements; the girl she saw in front of her met them all.

She was beginning to be saddened by this mental comparison and resolved to go about her business when she spotted him. He was extremely tall, dressed expensively in a black doublet and black cloak, and had a shiny black beard which was neatly trimmed. His hawk-like nose was pointed at his prey as though he were about to pounce. Jasmine followed his eyes to discover the object of his fascination and found that it was the same girl she herself had been watching.

She would, of course, have expected a man to be watching so pretty a girl as this, but something about his stare told her to be wary. She watched as he followed the girl who had removed a lovely pink pouch from her belt and was about to purchase a brooch from a stall not far from where Jasmine was standing. He took a step toward her, only to stop suddenly as another man raced forward and grabbed the girl's pouch, knocking her down in the process. He ran after the thief and Jasmine soon lost sight of them both among the crowd.

She looked for the girl, who had already been helped up and ushered into one of the shops, leaving Jasmine feeling breathless and bewildered. What had she just witnessed? A theft, certainly. But there seemed to be more to it than that. What were the odds of two men stalking the same girl at the same time in a crowded marketplace? York was known for its vandals, but she had never seen anything like this. She began to walk in the direction of The Shambles, the apples for the tart forgotten, wanting nothing more than to be in the safety and comfort of her own small home.

Chapter Three

Bess knelt in the south chapel of Holy Trinity Church, said a silent prayer before proceeding to the Cardwell family crypt. She went to the familiar spot where her mother was laid to rest, and hesitantly touched the cold, white marble stone. If only her mother were still alive! Things would be so different. She would have a friend, someone she could confide in, who would love her unconditionally. How she longed for that!

She began to tell her mother about her life, about how wretched she felt now that her father had married again. She told her about the shocking events of yesterday, the theft of her pouch and distress to her person. The young under-sheriff who had come to talk to her about the incident had told her that he would keep her informed on whether or not they caught the thief and recovered her pouch. She didn't hold much hope of recovery, however, especially considering her luck during the past week. It seemed to Bess that even God was against her, and she felt more alone than ever. She crossed herself before exiting the chapel and proceeded through the churchyard.

She enjoyed walking through the maze of gravestones, especially on a cloudy, windy autumn day like today and she pulled up her hood, comforting her face with its fur-lined warmth. Bess spotted a girl who looked to be her own age kneeling at a grave site and approached her. She saw her get up slowly, turning slightly so that Bess could see her face under her hood. She recognized her as the girl who had knocked her down over a week ago.

Bess found that her anger and frustration had not been eased by confiding them to her long-dead mother, now let that anger loose upon the girl by saying, "It is you again! Not playing football with your peasant friends, I see. I will be talking to the sheriff soon. I wonder what he would think of your game and the fact that you assaulted me?"

She garnered no response from the girl with that threat, so she tried another, "Or perhaps I should tell your father?"

To Bess' delight, she found that her remark had hit its target as the girl clutched at the gravestone in front of her. She began to walk haughtily past her, casting a sideways glance at the girl through narrowed eyes. What she saw made her pause, however, before continuing on the road home. There were tears in the girl's eyes. Surely she was not as thin-skinned as that? She turned back toward the churchyard in time to see the girl running away as fast as she could.

Bess felt a slight pang in her chest, knowing that she was to blame for the other girl's tears. She retraced her steps and found herself in front of the gravestone where the girl had been kneeling. Reading the inscription, she felt tears well up in her own eyes as she whispered, "God forgive me! What have I done?"

Jasmine ran all the way home from the churchyard, stopping only because Harry had grabbed her and told her to meet him that night at Vespers. She had continued without uttering a word, leaving Harry looking bewildered, concern for his friend showing upon his face.

She managed to sneak into her house without her father noticing, as he was cutting an exceptionally large piece of mutton at the time, and went up the cramped stairs to the third floor which held her father's bedchamber. She went to the window and looked out onto the busy street below. Her eyes still stung from her tears and from the cold, and she wiped them with the sleeve of her gown. This action made her think of her mother, who would have scolded her for being so childish and given her a hankerchief to use instead.

She spotted her mother's old coffer-chest and opened its lid slowly. Inside she saw a few of her mother's gowns and a pouch that she knew held her mother's only jewelry: a brooch made of silver, a crucifix chain, and her wedding ring. She rummaged through the coffer until she found what she was looking for, an old piece of finely embroidered cloth, which was wrapped around a small brown bottle. She unfolded the linen, removed the stopper, and breathed deeply of its contents. The sweet smell of Jasmine filled her with memories of her mother, who had loved to wear this perfume on special occasions, had even named her only daughter after its fragrance. New tears began to flow down Jasmine's cheeks and she let them out now, sobbing uncontrollably as she knelt on the hard wooden floor.

It seemed like a long time before her tears stopped and she was able to compose herself again. Jasmine now sat on the window seat, clutching her knees to her chest. Once again she looked down at the bustle of The Shambles and began to feel better. This was her home, these were the people she knew and who were a part of her life. She spotted Mrs. Stopplewick walking hurriedly down the street. She must have been buying meat from Papa, Jasmine thought, and smiled.

Her gaze was then interrupted by the figure of another person walking toward their shop, and

Jasmine froze at the sight of her. It was that girl again! Did she really mean to tell Papa about her football playing? She ran downstairs in the attempt to intercept the girl before she could speak to her father. She was too late.

Bess stood at the doorstep of the shop and asked the butcher if his daughter was at home. She noticed that the first floor of the house served as part of the butcher's shop, with a stall in front of the building set up so that he could cut and display the meat.

Mr. Bowles was surprised that a girl of such obvious high birth would be asking for his daughter, but welcomed her heartily and led her up the stairs to the family's living quarters.

Bess stepped into the small room and noticed that it served both as a solar, or sitting room, and as a dining room. There was a window seat to her left, a settle resting close to the brazier, a chest, and a trestle table toward the back of the room on which Bess assumed they ate.

Mr. Bowles offered her a seat on the settle and told her he would fetch his daughter.

Jasmine had retreated to her bedchamber, hoping to stall the inevitable for as long as possible. When her father entered her chamber, she started to explain, "Papa, I know..."

Mr. Bowles interrupted her by saying, "Jasmine dear, you have company. There's a lovely girl out there who says she's a friend of yours."

When Jasmine didn't move, he continued, "Perhaps she would like some ale and one of your sweet cakes."

"Yes, Papa," Jasmine responded as she entered the main room and saw the girl sitting patiently on the settle, looking nothing like the cold-hearted rich girl she had encountered in the churchyard.

When Jasmine emerged with the cakes, Mr. Bowles said, "Well, I have my shop to attend to. You'll excuse me, ladies?"

Bess stood and smiled as the rotund man squeezed down the narrow stairway. She immediately went to the table where Jasmine had laid out the sweet cakes and was pouring them both a cup of ale.

As Jasmine poured the ale, proud of its fine quality, she was thankful that they could afford such luxury. Only the poorest of the poor drank water, and even though they were not affluent enough to offer wine to her quest, she knew that the ale would do quite nicely.

Bess looked at her and said, "I came here to apologize for my behavior toward you."

Jasmine was so shocked she nearly dropped one of the cups onto the floor. She looked at the girl who seemed to be sincere and could not believe her good fortune. "You are very kind, Miss," she acknowledged, and motioned for her to be seated.

"My name is Elizabeth Cardwell, but my friends call me Bess," she told her, and Jasmine did not know whether this was said as an invitation or merely information for future reference.

"I'm Jasmine Bowles," she replied sheepishly. She had never entertained a person of Bess' class before and did not know how to proceed.

Bess tasted one of the sweet cakes and remarked that they were very good.

"Thank you," Jasmine said, then realized that another apology was in order. "I, too, would like to apologize for running into you the other day. I hope you weren't hurt very badly?"

"Not at all. Although you gave my maid some mending work to do on that gown!" She noticed Jasmine's face turn red and quickly added, "Do not worry, it was not one of my favorites, and Maude certainly needed the extra activity! Alice always tells me that I do not keep her as busy as I ought."

"Who's Alice?" Jasmine inquired, then saw Bess' face change in an instant and wished she hadn't asked.

"Alice is my father's new wife," she answered plainly.

Jasmine didn't brooch the matter further, instead asked if she would like some more ale.

Bess was not accustomed to the taste of ale, much preferred wine, but didn't wish to be rude and said, "Yes, please."

After Jasmine had refilled her cup, Bess decided to steer the conversation toward the matter she was most curious about and said, "I saw your mother's gravestone. This must be a difficult time for you."

Jasmine cleared her throat, did not want Bess to hear the anquish in her voice and tried to reply as steadily as she could. "Yes. It was one year ago today that my Mama died. She got sick. It was all so sudden. It seemed as though one day she was here, the next she was gone."

Bess saw the hurt that Jasmine tried to hide, wished that she had something to say to ease the pain, but knew that words would not help.

Jasmine changed the subject by asking, "What were you doing at the church? I have never seen you there before."

"When we are residing in town, we normally attend All Saints Church, but the Cardwell family has long had a crypt at Holy Trinity." She cleared her throat before adding, "My mother is buried there."

Jasmine was shocked by this revelation. "How long ago did your mother pass away?"

"Over thirteen years now. She died in childbirth. The baby was stillborn and my mother never recovered her health, died only a few weeks after that."

"I'm so sorry."

Bess nodded her head, did not know what else to say.

"Is that what brought you here? Sympathy for my loss because you, too, lost your mother?" Jasmine surprised Bess by asking.

"I suppose so," she acknowledged, but wanted to let Jasmine know that that was not the only reason for her visit.

"When I saw your mother's grave, I suddenly became aware of how selfish I have been lately. I realized for the first time in a long time that there are other people in the world who have needs that are larger than mine. I had to come and tell you how sorry I am, not only for my actions, but also for the loss of your mother."

Jasmine was touched, Bess had no need to reveal so much to her, but did anyway. She decided to lighten things a bit by asking, "How did you find out where I live?"

Bess smiled at the memory. "I tried to follow you, but you had such a headstart that I soon lost your trail. Then I came upon one of the boys that I had seen playing football with you, and asked him where you lived. He would not tell me at first, made me swear that I had no intention of causing you trouble."

"Harry?"

"That was his name, I believe, yes."

"Good old Harry, faithful as a watchdog."

"You are fortunate to have such a friend," Bess told her, and Jasmine could hear the envy in her voice.

Then she remembered having seen the strange man dressed in black following Bess in the marketplace and told her all about him.

"Are you certain he was following me?" Bess asked.

"Quite certain," Jasmine exclaimed. "I felt sure he was about to do you harm, possibly steal your pouch, before the real thief made off with it, that is."

"I can't imagine why anyone would be following me," Bess said, truly puzzled by this revelation.

Jasmine looked toward the window, noticed the deepening color of the sky and said, "You'd best be getting home before it gets dark."

Bess was quick to agree and thanked her for the sweet cakes and ale.

Jasmine walked her to the door and said, "Thank you so much for coming. And be careful on the way home, Elizabeth."

Bess stepped into the street, turned and said, "I told you, my friends do call me Bess."

Jasmine smiled as she watched her new friend walk quickly down the crowded street and out of sight.

Mr. Bowles finished the meal that Jasmine had prepared and exclaimed, "That was wonderful, my dear, wonderful!"

He had a way of repeating himself which Jasmine had always thought endearing. She had asked her father if she could hear Vespers at the church with

Harry to which he had enthusiastically approved. As she wrapped her cloak around her and headed down the stairs she felt a twinge of conviction however, knowing that Christian piety was not her reason for going. She knew that if Harry wanted to tell her something and was willing to endure Vespers in order to do so, it must be worth hearing!

Because the city of York had no ordinances requiring street lighting, Jasmine carried a lantern with her, holding it aloft with one hand and clutching her cloak tightly about her with the other. It had yet to rain, but Jasmine felt certain that it would soon; the air had that expectant feeling to it, and as it swirled about her she remembered the face of the strange man who had been watching Bess and shuddered. She was glad the walk to the church was a short one and felt relief as she stepped through the small, low vestibule.

She spotted the Stopplewicks sitting in their usual pew and slipped wordlessly beside Harry, who gave her a sly wink. After being greeted by his parents, she took a moment to view her surroundings. The familiar church had always been a favorite place of hers. It was made of stone, had beautiful arched windows and lovely tapestries on the walls depicting various Biblical events. The tower, which stood adjacent to the north aisle, was twice the height of the rest of the church and held a pack-saddle roof.

Jasmine's mother used to come here and view with wondrous eyes the ivory image of the virgin Mary, complete with a silver girdle. Jasmine now found herself blinking back tears; it had been some time since she had last set foot inside Holy Trinity, found the memories of her mother too raw to bear in the church she had so loved.

Once Vespers had been said the parishioners began to file out, and Harry told his parents he would like to escort Jasmine home.

"That is an excellent idea," exclaimed Mr. Stopplewick. He then said to Jasmine, "Be sure to tell your father a fine hello from us!"

Jasmine assured him that she would and started walking through the grassy churchyard with Harry. He wasted no time in telling her all about his news.

"You'll not believe what I found!" he said excitedly.

Jasmine waited for him to continue, then realized that he needed her to prompt him with, "What?"

"Five pounds!"

"Five pounds?" Jasmine repeated. That was a lot of money, and she knew that if Harry found it, someone else must be looking for it.

"Where on earth did you find five pounds?"

"I just happened to be around back of the blacksmith's shop last night and found a fellow in the stables." He waited for the proper second to pass for emphasis before adding, "He was dead."

Jasmine stopped in her tracks, turned to Harry and tried to clarify his statement by asking, "You found a dead man in the stables in back of the blacksmith's shop?"

When he nodded she said, "And you began this story by telling me about finding five pounds? Did you not think finding a dead body more important than that?"

"Not really. I have no use for a dead man, but five pounds? Can you imagine what we could buy with five pounds?"

"We?"

"Of course!"

"Won't our parents wonder where all this money suddenly came from?"

"Oh, we can spend it little by little, over time. No one need know anything about it," he explained. She wasn't taking his news like he had hoped. Why must girls analyze everything?

"Harry, let's go back for a moment. You say you found a dead body. Do you know who it was?"

"Can't say that I do. Some stranger in town, probably. What does it matter?"

"It just does," Jasmine answered, exasperated, wondering how he could be so nonchalant about a dead body.

"Could you tell how the man died?"

"Looked like he was stabbed. Got it right in the stomach, blood all over the place."

Jasmine winced, but continued, "So this was murder. I don't suppose you told the sheriff?"

"Don't be daft! Why would I want to tell the sheriff? He would ask all sorts of questions, though couldn't be any more than you're askin' now!"

Jasmine ignored his last remark. "Was there anything else there besides the money? The murder weapon, perhaps?"

"No weapon that I could see. There was a pink pouch, though, looked like a lady's, too. Course it had blood all over it, no use to anyone now."

Jasmine stopped and stared into the night sky, her thoughts racing. Could the dead man be the thief who stole Bess' pink pouch? If so, why had he been killed? Her first inclination told her that someone killed him for the money he had stolen, and her mind immediately suspected the strange man she had seen following Bess. But why would the killer then leave without taking the money? Perhaps he was scared off by a passer-by before being able to secure it; perhaps that passer-by had been Harry.

"Jasmine?"

Harry's voice brought her back into the present, back to the churchyard where she stood facing a long-time friend whom she now feared might be in danger.

"Harry, what if the killer saw you take the money? Now he'll be looking for you to give it back!"

"I hadn't thought of that," Harry said, slowly taking in the possible repercussions of his actions.

"Listen, I know the young lady to whom the pink pouch belonged; the money you took was hers. We must go to her first thing tomorrow and return it!"

"Give it back? I won't!" Harry stated unconvincingly.

Jasmine knew him too well to believe he wouldn't return the money to its rightful owner, knew he simply needed some time to get used to the idea.

They began walking again, each lost in their own separate thoughts; Jasmine wondering why Bess would be carrying around so much money, and Harry wondering why he had bothered to tell Jasmine about it in the first place.

When they reached Jasmine's house she instructed Harry, "Now you be here bright and early tomorrow with the money, you hear?"

"Yes," a downcast Harry replied, then skulked back to his own home as the sky began to pour.

Bess hadn't seen her brother all evening. Alice had informed her that her father had taken William to the Merchant Adventurers' Hall for his weekly meeting. This did not surprise Bess; ever since William had turned eighteen, his father had seen to it that he was more involved in the family business. Sir James was one of the most prominent members of the Wool Merchant's Guild, gaining more responsibility with each passing year. Bess would have been proud of that fact, except that it took her father away from her, both in body and in mind.

She waited in her bedchamber until she heard them arrive back home. Looking out her window, she could see her father and brother in the courtyard below dismounting their horses and handing them over to the grooms who would take them to the stables.

Throwing her dressing robe over her kirtle, Bess started downstairs in search of her brother. She found him in the great hall, talking with their father. As she approached, she could hear the strain in their voices as they spoke, and knew that something was amiss.

At sight of his daughter, Sir James said softly to his son, "We shall speak no more of this," and bade Bess to come toward them.

"Sorry if I am interrupting," she said hesitantly.

"Not at all, Bess," her father assured her. "Although I am bone-tired. I have had a long day. Good night to you both."

He patted his daughter's head before exiting the hall, and Bess noticed the look that passed between father and son.

"What have you been talking about?" she asked her brother.

"Nothing that concerns you, dearest," William said, stifling a yawn.

Bess thought that it concerned her greatly, but did not press the matter, instead began to tell him of her experience that day. She told him all about Jasmine, seeing her in the churchyard, visiting her home, telling her she was sorry.

"I feel different Will," she tried to explain.

"How?" he inquired.

"I feel happy again. After apologizing to Jasmine, I found that it was easier to apologize to God and repented of my horrible actions lately. It is as if a tremendous weight has been lifted from me."

"That is wonderful, Bess!" William exclaimed, glad that something good came of this day. He then noticed the silver crucifix chain that hung from her neck.

"I see you are wearing mother's crucifix again."

"Yes," she replied, as she took the cross and held it tightly between both hands.

Jasmine found Harry on her doorstep the next morning, just as she had asked.

"I was not sure you would show up," she teased.

"Don't laugh. I almost didn't!"

"Let's go then," she prompted, leading him by the arm.

"How do you know where this girl lives?" he asked.

"My father knows of Cardwell Hall. He told me how to get there," she explained. "Any more questions?"

"Yes one. Do I have to go?" he pleaded.

"Of course you have to go! You found the money and took it, now it is up to you to return it."

"But my father is not feeling well today. He needs me to work in the shop."

Jasmine noticed that he could not look her in the eyes, thought to mention that his father seemed in fine health just the night before, but instead shook her head helplessly.

"I cannot force you to go," she finally told him.

"I know," he said, suddenly in good spirits. "Here's the money," he stated, thrusting a brown leather pouch in front of her, adding, "I want it back; that, at least, is mine!"

Jasmine took the pouch, thought better than to ask him if all the money was there, knew the question would offend him terribly. Her friend may be a thief, but he was certainly not a cheat.

The clouds of the previous night had blown away and the city looked new and clean in the bright morning sun. Jasmine had no trouble finding Cardwell Hall, which was large enough to contain a dozen or more small houses like hers inside its walls.

She approached the large, double front doors with trepidation, but before she could reach them, one of the servants came running up to her.

"Can I help you?" he asked, looking her up and down.

"I'm here to see Bess," she began, before checking herself. "I mean to say, Miss Elizabeth Cardwell."

"Are you a friend of hers?" he asked, obviously suspicious of that fact.

"Yes. Well, I just met her yesterday and…"

He took her arm and said, "I think you'd better come with me, Miss."

"Where are you taking me?" she demanded, knowing she could free herself of his grip with one motion if she desired.

"Around to the servants' entrance. Then we will see if you are indeed a friend of the young lady's."

Jasmine allowed him to take her to the back of the house. They entered through a small door into the huge kitchen. She took in all the activity; cooks baking bread and preparing the morning meal, servants going in and out, busy with their various chores. No one stopped to pay much attention to her and she realized that in appearance she could be taken for any one of them.

The man motioned for her to sit in a chair which was in the corner, out of the way, and she did so, clutching the leather pouch tightly in her hands. He seemed to be gone for quite some time and she wondered if she had been mistaken in coming, mistaken in calling Bess a friend.

The swinging door that led to the kitchen opened slowly and the man, looking sufficiently chastised, said, "Miss Elizabeth will see you now. If you'll come with me?"

Jasmine followed him through the great hall, which had stone floors and whitewashed walls on which hung beautifully decorated tapestries, into a large, welcoming chamber containing a huge hearth. Nestled closely by the hearth were two settles and a small table. A large sideboard sat on the right-hand side of the room, along with a writing desk, neatly organized.

She noticed the tall, rounded windows on the wall directly opposite her, and saw that perched below in one of the cozy window seats was Bess, who rose instantly to greet her guest.

"Jasmine! What a pleasant surprise," she exclaimed as she grasped Jasmine's hand and led her to the settle, bidding her to sit down.

"Are you hungry or thirsty?" Bess asked and, not waiting for a response, said to the servant, "Please bring us some bread, cheese, and wine."

She looked curiously at Jasmine. "What brings you here?"

"I'm sorry to call on you so early, but I have important news about the theft of your pouch."

Bess' eyes widened. "Did they catch the thief?"

"In a way," Jasmine responded, hoping to keep her friend Harry out of this as much as possible. "I believe the man who stole your pouch was found murdered in the blacksmith's stables."

"No!" Bess, exclaimed, her hands covering her mouth in disbelief.

"But the good news is this," she said, lifting up the leather pouch. "Your money has been recovered!"

"That is good news," she agreed, not wanting to quench Jasmine's enthusiasm. Her money did not matter when compared to a man's life, even if that man was a thief.

Jasmine poured the coins into Bess' hands, and watched as her face grew more and more confused as each coin slipped from the pouch.

"Whatever is the matter?" she asked.

Bess could not believe what she held. "I did not have this much money with me when my pouch was stolen. I could not have had more than a few pence, to be sure."

"Are you certain?" Jasmine asked, not because she doubted Bess' words, but because she could not believe what she was hearing.

"Quite certain. Where did this money come from?"

Jasmine realized she would have to tell her the whole story, including Harry's part in it, and hoped that Bess would not inform anyone else.

"My friend Harry, whom you've met, found the dead man's body and retrieved the money. He told me about it last night and mentioned that he saw a pink pouch lying beside the body. I instantly realized that this must be the man who stole your pouch, and convinced Harry to return the money to its rightful owner."

"Then where is he?"

Jasmine was surprised by this question, but did not blame her for asking it. "Harry's father fell ill, leaving Harry to run the family business in his absence, but he did ask me to give you his regards."

Bess was satisfied with that answer, though she did not necessarily believe it. "Did Harry tell the sheriff about the body?"

Jasmine blushed, knew that that should have been the first thing to be done. "Not that I'm aware," she responded truthfully.

Both girls fell silent, each thinking about the strange turn of events. The servant came in with the bread, cheese and wine, and Bess poured them both a cup.

Jasmine had not had much experience drinking wine; it was too expensive for her family's everyday use. She sipped it cautiously and found it to be rather sour for her taste. The bread and cheese was a welcome addition, however, and she ate it thankfully as she pondered the turn of events. If Bess hadn't had five pounds in her pouch at the time it was stolen, then where did the money come from? And why did the thief steal Bess' pouch to begin with?

Their thoughts were interrupted by the entrance of William into the solar. He was accompanied by the under-sheriff who had spoken with Bess directly after the theft two days ago.

"Bess, there you are," William began, then seeing Jasmine said, "Oh, I see you have a visitor. Perhaps she will excuse us; the sheriff has some news to relate about your stolen pouch."

Jasmine rose to leave, but Bess stopped her and said, "Will, this is my friend Jasmine. Whatever the kind sheriff wishes to tell me, she can hear as well."

William began to protest, but the sheriff interrupted by introducing himself to Jasmine.

"My name is Thomas Wainwright," he told her quickly. Having much to do today already, he had no intention of being overly delayed by a family squabble. "What I've come to report is that we found the man who stole your pouch, Miss," he said, directing his words toward Bess.

Jasmine stole a glance at her friend, hoping she would not mention anything about Harry's involvement.

"Where did you find him?" Bess asked, quickly returning Jasmine's gaze.

"In the stables behind the blacksmith's shop. He'd been killed, victim of a theft himself it seems, since the money he stole from you was nowhere to be found. We did recover this, however," he said, holding the pink pouch out to her.

It was covered in blood and Bess did not want to touch it, but also did not want to appear childish to the handsome sheriff. He was not much older than her brother; Bess judged him to be in his early twenties. He was of medium height and build, with brown hair that almost touched his shoulders. Bess looked into his eyes and thought they were the most beautiful shade of green she had ever seen. She was grateful when William said, "Sheriff, please set that on the table and I will have our laundress try to remove the stain, though I cannot say I hold much hope of that."

Jasmine could not resist asking, "Was anything else found at the scene of the crime besides the pouch?"

The sheriff could not hide his surprise at the impertinence of her question, but found it to be curious since there had indeed been another item recovered.

"Why yes, we did find something else; a torn piece of paper clutched in the victim's hand."

"Could you distinguish if anything was written on it?" she asked.

"Just the word No," he told her.

"Do you have any idea who might have killed him?" she questioned further.

"No, and I really don't expect to. Thief killing another thief, not the sort of thing we spend a lot of time looking into." He directed his next words at Bess. "In fact, I want to apologize for not bringing over your pouch yesterday directly after we found the body, but we've been quite busy. It gets this way every year before Hallowmas, especially for an under-sheriff like myself."

Convinced that he had been as obliging as possible, Thomas bid them farewell and exited the chamber.

Jasmine and Bess looked at each other conspiratorially. William noticed this exchanged glance and asked, "What is it?"

"Whatever do you mean, Will?" Bess responded playfully. She then remembered her manners and introduced her brother to Jasmine.

"Nice to make your acquaintance," she said, hoping to appear calm.

Jasmine was anything but comfortable, however, in the company of William Cardwell. All she could think of was that the first time he had seen her she had been playing football, her gown tied up around her knees, her face smudged with dirt, and her hair in a wild mess. Jasmine hoped that she presented a more civilized appearance this morning, although she somehow doubted it. She saw that William was quite like his sister in many ways; he was as fair as she, had the same blue eyes, but Jasmine thought him to be almost a foot taller than Bess.

Before he could question them further, Alice appeared in the doorway with Margaret. She was obviously surprised by Jasmine's presence.

"And who might this be?" she asked.

"This is my friend Jasmine," Bess responded. "Jasmine, this is my father's wife, Alice, and their daughter Margaret."

Jasmine could not help but notice the faint hint of animosity in Bess' voice, wondered if Alice noticed it, too. If she did, she did not let on, for she smiled broadly at Jasmine and said, "Welcome to my home."

Bess announced that she and Jasmine were going to stroll through the gardens and before Jasmine could blink, they were out of the house and walking along a path of crushed rock.

"Did you hear what she said?" Bess asked, anger showing upon her face.

Jasmine did not think she needed to reply, and was proven correct.

"Welcoming you to *her* home! The nerve of that woman!" Bess kicked at an unsuspecting rock, sending it flying through the flower beds.

"I'm sure she did not mean it as such," Jasmine offered. "After all, she does live here, too."

Bess realized how petty she must sound, did not want to present an unfavorable impression to her new friend, so she changed the subject.

"You seemed to be quite interested in the piece of paper found in the thief's hand. You were very bold to ask the sheriff about it; I daresay I would not have had as much courage!"

"I learned early in life that I can't read minds; if I want to know something, I find it helps greatly to ask!" Jasmine replied good-naturedly. She had always been outspoken; in truth, she did not know how to behave any other way. "But speaking of the note," Jasmine continued, "do you not realize what it means?"

Bess looked at her blankly.

"The thief was paid the five pounds in exchange for the note, I am sure of it!"

Bess' mind went to work, "But if he received the five pounds and his . . .contact, shall we say, received the note, then why was the thief killed?"

"I believe it to be very telling that a torn piece of the note was found clutched in the thief's hand, as though he had been unwilling to part with it. Perhaps he was trying to garner more money before handing over the note. Perhaps there was a struggle and the contact stabbed the thief, then tore the piece of paper from his hand and fled."

Both girls were deep in thought, trying to digest the implications of their theory.

Bess stopped and, hoping it would not seem a stupid question, asked, "Where did the thief get the note?"

"From your pouch!" Jasmine answered excitedly.

"My pouch?" Bess exclaimed. "But I did not put it there! How could it possibly have come from my pouch?"

"Someone must have put the note inside your pouch in anticipation of the thief stealing it."

"That does not make sense. How could anyone know my pouch would be stolen?"

"What if this person told the thief ahead of time that there would be a note in your pouch and to retrieve it from you when you went to the marketplace?"

"So you are saying that the thief stole my pouch not for my money, but for the note it contained."

"Exactly!"

"It certainly seems to be a strange way to deliver a note, and quite hazardous as well. Who would concoct such a scheme, if indeed we are correct?" Bess asked.

"I admit it does appear rather far-fetched," Jasmine acknowledged. "On the other hand, it seems to be the only explanation for the theft. If the thief already had the note, and planned to receive five pounds for it, he would hardly need to steal your pouch, would he?"

"Jasmine, you are forgetting one thing – he was a thief. People who steal do so for many reasons; we cannot hope to know their motivation."

Jasmine could not suppress a smirk for she knew Bess to be right. She had only to think of Harry to provide an example of Bess' words. He certainly had no reason to steal; he did it solely for the excitement, and possibly because he could not help himself. How she prayed that he would mend his ways before he met with the same fate that had befallen the thief.

She shuddered at the thought and said quickly, "What you say is true, however if my theory, however unlikely, proves to be correct, then someone you trust deliberately put you in danger in order to deliver a message to an unknown person. We simply cannot ignore that!"

Bess felt her head begin to ache and rubbed her temples. This was too much to contemplate!

Where do you keep your pouch?" Jasmine asked.

"In my coffer. But wait! The morning of the theft, I went to retrieve my pouch from my coffer but it was not there!"

"Where was it?"

"It was in the solar; Alice pointed it out to me." Bess remembered the incident and froze, chills running down her spine.

Jasmine noticed the look on her face and asked, "Do you think Alice could have put the note in your pouch?"

"I am sure of it! Now that I think back on that morning, I remember that Alice forbade me to go into town that day."

Jasmine did not understand the significance of this and said, "But if she did not want you to go into town, then she must not have known about the note."

"Do you not see?" Bess asked impatiently. "Alice knows that I always do the opposite of what she tells me! It has been that way for the past three years; surely she knew it would be the same that morning!"

Chapter Four

Jasmine returned to her home, her mind racing after the events of the morning. If she was right, a man had been killed for the information found on a note that had been placed inside Bess' pouch, information that had come from someone in Bess' own household. She knew that Bess was convinced that Alice was the person responsible, and Jasmine had pointed out to her that anyone in the Cardwell home could have put the note inside her pouch, but she would not listen. Jasmine hoped that Bess would not do anything foolish, had made her promise not to mention anything to anyone until they met later that day.

Jasmine found her father sitting at the table, his head in his hands.

"Papa, what's wrong?" she asked, afraid of what the answer might be. "Why are you not downstairs in the shop?"

"Let the people buy from someone else today," he said, not looking at his daughter.

Jasmine crossed the room and went to his side. "Are you sick? Would you like some of Mrs. Stopplewick's special tea?"

"No, my dear. I am not sick, just very tired. I didn't get much sleep last night. I think I'll go back to bed. I just wanted to make sure you got home first," he explained, patting Jasmine's hand.

She knew why he had not slept last night, understood that he had been thinking of her mother and had probably been crying just as she herself had been. Why they could not share their grief, she did not know, but it had always been that way.

"Sleep well, Papa. I'll be here when you wake up, will make us some stew and fresh bread," she offered.

"Thank you, my dear," he replied as he began the climb upstairs to his bedchamber.

Jasmine was left alone to prepare the meal and to think, but instead of dwelling on the sadness she and her father felt, she was thankfully now able to focus her thoughts elsewhere. Someone in the Cardwell household had put a note inside Bess' pouch, intending for it to be stolen and then sold to another mysterious person. But why? Why not simply inform the person directly? Perhaps it would have been too dangerous or difficult for them to be seen together. Alice suddenly flew into Jasmine's mind. She did not want to jump to conclusions, however, and forced herself to think of other possibilities.

She tried, only to recall the image of the strange man in black she had seen in the marketplace. What did he have to do with all of this, if anything? He had gone after the thief. Perhaps he had caught up with him, struggled to gain possession of the note, and killed the thief in the process. But that did not explain the extra five pounds found near the body. Jasmine did not think the man in black would have tried to buy the note; he did not look the type who would purchase what he could take by force.

Her thoughts were interrupted by a loud knock on the door. She went downstairs to answer it and found Harry, disheveled and out of breath.

"Harry, what on earth is the matter? Come inside, quickly!" Jasmine instructed her friend.

Once he was comfortably seated on the settle and fresh coals were heaped upon the brazier, Jasmine asked him what had happened.

"Mother and I had gone to the marketplace...when we got back...our house had been pillaged!" he sputtered, noticeably shaken by what had happened.

Jasmine grabbed Harry's hand, tried to sooth his nerves.

"What do you mean by pillaged?"

"I mean that someone had gone through our things, made a huge mess that Mother is even now trying to sort out!"

"Was anything stolen?" she asked.

"Mother thinks not. We don't have much to steal, as you well know, and the few pieces of jewelry Mother does own were not taken."

Jasmine was touched by Harry's present emotional state. Never had she seen him so vulnerable. His carefree attitude and jaunty outlook on life had been replaced by something which Jasmine had never beheld in her long-time friend - fear.

"Let me get you some ale," she offered.

"Thank you, but no," he said. "I have to get back. Mother wants me at home with her for the rest of the day, but I had to come over and tell you what had happened first."

"I'm glad you did. Tell your mother if there is anything I can do, just let me know."

"I will," he said as he rose from the settle. "By the way, where is your father today? I noticed that his shop is not open. Is anything amiss?"

"Oh no, he is simply not feeling well. Nothing serious."

Harry smiled, said goodbye, and was down the stairs and out the door before Jasmine could tell him to be careful on the way home.

She had not told him of her own fears, that his house might have been ransacked because someone was searching for something. The missing five pounds, perhaps? But she had said nothing; he had worries enough without her adding to them. Besides, she could be mistaken.

She suddenly felt very cold and went to the window to close the shutters. She could see Harry as he turned the corner, heading home. She grabbed hold of the shutters and began to close them, only to stop immediately when she saw someone else turn down the same street as Harry had, someone she recognized, someone who confirmed her worst fears...the man in black.

Jasmine crept out of the house, not wanting to disturb her father, and silently closed the front door. Once safely outside, she ran as fast as she could down the street, turning the same corner as Harry and the man in black had, then slowed to a walk and kept her eyes open, searching for a glimpse of them. She could see nothing, however, and continued on, walking briskly and hoping for the best.

She turned down Petergate just in time to see Harry entering his house. With a sigh of relief, Jasmine now concentrated on finding the man she had seen following Harry as he left her house. She kept to the right-side of the crowded street, walking as nonchalantly as she could, her eyes searching for a tall man dressed all in black.

She passed Harry's house and still did not see him, so she decided to give up and go back to her own house; she had a stew to make for her father.

She turned around quickly and felt a man's strong hands grip her shoulders in an effort to keep her from bumping into him. She looked up, recognized him in an instant, and felt chills run up and down her spine.

"You ought to be more careful where you tread, Miss," he said in a low, husky voice.

Jasmine was acutely aware of his steel grey eyes as they searched her own, still felt his hands on her shoulders.

"Sorry, sir," she mumbled as she quickly stepped aside to let him pass.

Jasmine watched as he continued to walk down the street, pausing only to take a quick glance at Harry's house, then back at Jasmine, before disappearing out of sight.

After their regular noon-time dinner, Bess was alone in the solar with Alice, who was busying herself with a piece of embroidery. Bess held her own needlework in her lap, trying to concentrate on her stitches. When she poked herself for the third time, however, she finally gave up, went to the hearth to warm her hands by the fire.

Alice did not stir, but said in an even voice, "It was interesting to meet your new friend this morning."

Bess did not like the sound of that and questioned, "What do you mean by 'interesting', Madame?"

"Nothing. It is just that I would have expected you to cultivate a friendship more suitable to your position."

"I happen to believe that any friendship is suitable to my position if I deem it so," she said carefully.

"Come now, Elizabeth, surely you do not expect me to agree that that girl is an appropriate companion for you?"

Bess felt a rush of anger flood her cheeks. "Her name is Jasmine, and I do not require you to agree with me. In fact, I do not require anything of you at all, except perhaps, the truth."

"Whatever do you mean by that, Elizabeth?" Alice asked, putting down her embroidery.

Bess turned and confronted her stepmother. "When my pouch was missing two days ago, you knew exactly where it was, on the window seat in the solar. You said that I had left it there, did you not? Well, I think that you left it there, after you stole it from my coffer!"

"Why would I take your pouch?" she asked, an incredulous look spread upon her face.

"Do not feign innocence, Madame. I know that you put a note in my pouch, and that it contained information someone was willing to kill for! I do not have proof of your involvement yet, but be sure that when I do, Father will be the first to know!"

Bess stormed out of the solar, leaving Alice staring wide-eyed in disbelief.

William caught up with his sister as she was crossing the great hall, spun her around to face him.

"Where do you think you are going, little sister?" he asked, releasing his grip.

"I am going for a walk," she answered plainly.

"All alone? I think not. I shall accompany you," he said with mock gallantry in his voice.

"William, do please leave me alone!" Bess insisted.

"Not until you tell me where you are going and whom you are planning to meet."

"I am far too old for a nursemaid, although I do appreciate your concern," Bess replied sarcastically.

William was not about to let his sister go so easily, instead asked, "This new friend of yours – Jasmine, was it? I noticed that you spirited her away as quickly as possible this morning, before I could question her about what she had asked the sheriff. Could it be that the two of you know something that I do not?"

Bess rested her hands on her hips and said in an exasperated voice, "William Cardwell, if you are not the nosiest brother in Yorkshire! I thought you would be happy that I had made a new friend, instead you accuse me of deceit."

She pushed him out of her way. "Now if you will excuse me, I have an appointment that I wish to keep!"

William let her pass, knew there was more than one way to get the information he sought.

Jasmine was heartened by the pleased look on her father's face. They had finished their meal of fish stew and fresh bread she had prepared, and now her father pat his round belly and sighed contentedly.

"I'm glad to see that you're feeling better, Papa," Jasmine ventured.

"Aye. Nothing wrong that some sleep and a good meal could not cure," he said as he poured himself another cup of ale. "What were you up to today?"

"I finished mending Mr. Thompson's hose and laces, and began the tunic I am making for Mr. Sowers."

"Good girl!" he said, anticipating the extra money in his coffer. He got up from the table and announced, "Think I'll go to the Black Ox, see what's to-do over there."

Jasmine cringed. Whenever her father went to the Black Ox tavern, he spent too much money and came home smelling of ale, smoke, and sweat. She could hardly tell him not to go, instead reminded him to be home before the bells rang Compline.

"Aye, I will, I will," he assured her.

Once he had gone, Jasmine gathered her cloak, preparing to meet Bess in the churchyard as they had agreed. She was worried about Harry, however, and decided to pay the Stopplewicks a quick visit.

Mrs. Stopplewick opened the door just seconds after Jasmine knocked.

Jasmine could not help but see the disappointed look on her face that passed in an instant.

"Jasmine, dear, come in!" she invited.

"Thank you. I just wanted to come by and see how you are doing after the terrible events of this morning," she explained.

Harry came over and offered to take her cloak.

She declined, saying, "I really can't stay, I'm on my way to meet someone. I wondered if you've reported to the sheriff what happened?"

"I told the sheriff about it before I spoke with you this morning," Harry answered.

"Aye," said Mrs. Stopplewick, "and we haven't seen anything of him as yet. I thought, when you knocked..."

"I'm sorry I wasn't him," Jasmine offered, then asked Harry, "Which sheriff did you speak to?"

"Thomas Wainwright. The others said they were too busy. I'm sure that they just didn't think it was important enough to claim their attention."

There was a knock on the door and Mrs. Stopplewick rushed to answer it.

"Sheriff, come in, come in!" she offered, obviously relieved by his presence.

"I understand someone broke into your house this morning," he began, then stopped at sight of Jasmine. He gave her a quick nod of recognition and continued, "Was anything missing?"

"Not that I could tell," Mrs. Stopplewick answered. "My jewelry was the only thing of value in the house, and it was not taken. It seems he just made a big mess, and left."

Thomas took a turn around the room and said, "Well, it looks like everything has been put back in order. Since a theft has not actually occurred, there is not much that I can do. I would remind you to keep your doors and shutters locked in the future."

"But they were locked, sheriff!" Harry quickly told him. "My father had to repair the bolt on the door that had been damaged by the intruder."

Thomas appeared to be thinking about the situation, then said, "You will inform me if you discover that something has, in fact, been stolen?"

Mrs. Stopplewick nodded vigorously.

"Then I'll take my leave," the sheriff said as he turned and exited the house.

Jasmine told Mrs. Stopplewick to let her know if she needed anything mended, that she would be glad to help in any way she could, and Harry seemed pleased.

"That was kind of you," he remarked as he opened the door for her.

"It was nothing," she assured him, feeling a bit awkward. It was the first time she could ever remember Harry complimenting her. They smiled at each other briefly before she left the house.

She began walking in the direction of the churchyard when she heard from behind her, "Fancy meeting you again so soon."

Jasmine turned and saw the sheriff approaching her.

"Hello," was all she could think to say.

"You certainly are a busy girl. First I see you at Cardwell Hall this morning, and now here."

Jasmine's initial apprehension was replaced by relief when she saw the twinkle in his eyes, the slight curve of his lips.

"I could say the same of you," she responded, returning his smile. "I did want to ask you a question."

"You don't say?" he asked sarcastically.

She blushed, but continued, "Don't you think it strange that someone would go to all the trouble of breaking in a door, and then not steal anything?"

"Obviously you do," he stated, folding his arms across his chest.

"Yes, I do," she agreed.

She wanted to tell him that she thought Harry to be in danger, wanted to tell him of the strange man in black whom she had seen twice now, but found that she couldn't. She did not want to betray Harry, and that is what she would be doing if she confided in the sheriff. If she told him that she thought someone was trying to steal the five pounds from Harry, she would be announcing the fact that Harry had taken the money from the blacksmith's stables in the first place. It also occurred to her that she might inadvertently be implicating Harry in the murder of the thief.

So she said nothing more, and Thomas Wainwright seemed content with that.

"I don't want to see you at the scene of any more crimes today," he said, giving her a wink, and started to walk down the street.

Jasmine watched him for only a moment before heading to the churchyard to meet Bess.

Bess hated to be kept waiting. She assumed it was because she had had little experience of it, but wondered if it ever became less annoying. Pacing up and down in this silent churchyard, she somehow doubted it. She was immensely relieved, therefore, when she saw Jasmine's silhouette against the gravestone in front of her.

Turning, she announced, "I was just about to give up on you!"

"Sorry Bess. I wanted to see Harry before I met you. His house was broken into this morning," Jasmine revealed, hoping it would excuse her tardiness.

"Goodness!" Bess exclaimed. "Thievery is certainly running rampant in this city!"

"Actually, nothing was taken," Jasmine informed her.

"Thank God for that."

Jasmine leaned up against the gravestone. "I know this sounds strange, but I would prefer that something had been stolen."

"Why on earth would you wish that?"

"Because that would explain the break-in."

Bess noticed the troubled look on Jasmine's face and asked what was wrong.

"Bess, do you remember when I told you about the strange man in black that I saw following you?"

Bess nodded her head.

"I saw him again this morning, following Harry!"

Bess' eyes flew open wide. "Are you certain it was the same man?"

"Quite. After Harry came to my house I went after him, hoping to make sure no ill befell him, and inadvertently bumped into the man! Needless to say, I got a good look at him," Jasmine assured her, then remembering his cold eyes, added, "much too good for my taste!"

"Did he speak to you?"

"He told me I should be careful where I tread. I felt he was giving me a warning, as if he knew I had been looking for him."

"Do you think this man had something to do with Harry's house being broken into?"

"It's certainly a possibility."

"Perhaps he saw Harry at the scene of the murder and was trying to recover the stolen money," Bess offered.

"But then why would he not steal what he could while he was there? Mrs. Stopplewick said that she had some jewelry that had not been touched. Not the sort of behavior you would find in an ordinary thief, don't you agree?"

Bess had to admit that she did. But what other explanation could there be? There was a moment of silence as the girls thought about the situation, and Bess wondered if she should bring up her altercation with her stepmother, decided she had better.

"Jasmine, I know you told me not to talk to my stepmother about this, but..."

"Oh no," Jasmine began.

"Oh yes. I am truly sorry, but I could not help myself. My anger got the better of me once again," Bess explained.

"What did you say to her?"

"I told her that I knew she was the one who put the note in my pouch and that I would prove it to Father." She could not look Jasmine in the eyes.

Jasmine thought of the repercussions of this action and said, "If she did put the note in your pouch, then she now knows that we know, and will be doing what she can to cover her tracks. Although there is not much to link her with the act, the fact that the note contained a written message tells us that whoever wrote it had to be literate. That certainly warrants your stepmother being a suspect.

How many other people in your household can read and write?"

"Oh my! I have never bothered to think about that before. It certainly cannot be very many."

"We had better find out, don't you think?"

Bess agreed and they decided to proceed to Cardwell Hall to make the necessary inquiries.

Jasmine was again impressed by the scale of Bess' house in town. She could only wonder how magnificent their home in the country, Cardwell Manor, must be, but doubted she would ever see such a sight.

She followed Bess as they first questioned the outside servants including two grooms, and a stableboy. None knew how to write, although one groom told them that he could read. They proceeded indoors, first stopping in the kitchen to ask if any of the cooks could write, and found that one of them could, the baker. She was, not surprisingly, a round woman, with a jolly face that was quick to smile.

"Aye, I can write," she said, "and read, too."

She was in the middle of kneading a piece of dough with a ferocity that Jasmine found to be curious.

"Do you ever have occasion to go into any of the upstairs rooms?" Jasmine ventured.

The baker looked perplexed. "Why would I want to go upstairs? If I were even seen in the family quarters I'd be fired on the spot!"

Jasmine shot a glance at Bess, who didn't look as though she had just heard anything out of the ordinary, and wondered if Bess even knew the name of the woman who baked her bread every day.

"Well, thank you, Mrs. ..." Jasmine began, hoping for a name.

"Mrs. Sparger," the baker offered.

"Thank you, Mrs. Sparger," Jasmine repeated.

She had serious doubts that this woman could be responsible for the note, and told Bess so at the first opportunity.

"I quite agree," she said, "although you realize this still leaves Alice as the prime suspect?"

"I will defer my judgment until I've heard from all your servants. Just how many more are there?" Jasmine asked playfully.

"Oh, just the household servants are left; our personal maids and valets, and the serving staff, of course."

"Of course," Jasmine said, bowing her head slightly.

Bess smiled and said, "I cannot help the fact that we have servants, Jasmine. You should stay here with me for a week or so, just to see how helpful they can be."

"I have no doubt of that! I've often wished that I didn't have to prepare all the meals at my house. I do find it strange that you have a personal maid, though. Do you not despair of your privacy?"

"I can summon or discharge Maude as I wish," Bess explained. "Besides, if I did not employ Maude, she would have no other way of making a living. We are doing a great deal of good for the people who serve us."

"When you put it that way, I suppose I cannot argue," Jasmine said, although she knew that she could never bear to be anyone else's servant. Just the thought of it made her cringe, and she felt lucky to have her father to take care of her.

As Bess and Jasmine made their way through Cardwell Hall, they asked every servant they came across whether or not they could write, including Bess' personal maid, Maude.

"Yes, Miss. And I can read a bit, too. My fella's teaching me," she was proud to say.

They were in Bess' bedchamber, Maude having been stoking the fire when they found her, and Jasmine could not help but notice Bess' shocked expression when she learned that Maude could read and write.

"You were with me two days ago when I could not find my pouch. Do you remember?" Bess asked her maid.

"Yes, Miss. I guessed you found it because when you met me in the courtyard you had it tied to your belt."

"Do you know where I found it?"

"No, Miss," Maude answered, with a puzzled look on her face.

Bess did not know what else to ask, looked to Jasmine for help.

"Maude, can you think of anyone who could have taken Bess' pouch from her coffer?" Jasmine asked.

Maude put her hand to her chin, as if striking a thoughtful pose. "Aye, any of the personal servants could have, they're the ones up here in the family quarters all the time."

Bess and Jasmine both looked at Maude, then saw her face light up with recognition, as though understanding for the first time what they were accusing her of.

"If you think that I was the one who took your pouch, Miss... I didn't! Honest!"

Bess looked into Maude's eyes and could not tell if they held the fear of being wrongly accused, or the fear of discovery. Still, she could not bring herself to believe her own maid capable of such a thing.

"Do not worry, Maude, no one is blaming you. You may go now."

Maude made a hurried exit, and Bess and Jasmine plopped down upon the window seat, exhausted from their inquiries.

Jasmine was the first to speak. "I need not tell you that the list of suspects has just dwindled down to three."

"Mrs. Sparger, Maude, and Alice," Bess finished for her.

"We both agree that Mrs. Sparger is most likely innocent. She had not the opportunity, since she is in the kitchens all the time, and she doesn't strike me as the sort of person to be involved in any sort of intrigue," Jasmine pointed out.

Bess continued the analysis, "And Maude had the opportunity, for she is in this room constantly."

"I have a question," Jasmine interrupted. "Who knew you were going to the market that day?"

"Everyone knows that I go to the market on Wednesdays. It is no secret," Bess answered.

"So both Maude and Alice knew you would be going out on Wednesday, and where you would be. Both had the opportunity to slip the note in your pouch at any time before your excursion."

Bess rose and went to the four-poster bed, wrapping her arms around one of the posts. "You know I love my stepmother not, nevertheless, I cannot help but think that Alice fits perfectly into the role of prime suspect."

Jasmine was not about to convict Alice on the basis of Bess' jaded viewpoint however, and replied, "One thing is certain, neither one will confess. We must look at this from a new perspective. I keep thinking about the man in black. He is involved in this somehow, I am sure of it."

"But if he is as dangerous as you portray him to be, however can we discover whether he is or not?"

"Perhaps we can find someone who knows of him, knows what he is up to," Jasmine offered, not quite sure of her suggestion.

"But who?"

"If he is a stranger in town, he must be frequenting the local taverns for food and drink. We can question the proprietor, or perhaps a serving maid has noticed him. He is, after all, not the sort of man who would blend in with the woodwork!"

Jasmine saw Bess smile and was impressed by her own resourcefulness. She had to admit that she was enjoying this immensely, apart from the danger it might bring. But she pushed those thoughts aside, and suggested to Bess that they begin their inquiries as soon as possible.

Bess went to the window and peered through the glass.

"It looks as though we have a few hours of daylight left. Shall we go?"

Chapter Five

The first tavern Jasmine and Bess found was located on Fossgate, not far from Cardwell Hall. They were reluctant to enter, however, and spent a few moments outside questioning whether or not their venture was a prudent one.

"Jasmine, I have something to confess," Bess began sheepishly. "I have never actually been inside a tavern before."

Jasmine tried to keep from laughing at the girl's confession, knowing it was meant in all seriousness. The thought of Bess inside a tavern, however, brought a smile to her lips she could not suppress.

"Don't worry. I've been inside a few. Just follow close behind me and try not to look conspicuous."

Bess wanted to ask Jasmine the particulars of her experiences inside taverns, but decided it was none of her business. She did as Jasmine bade, and followed her through the door of the establishment.

The smell of liquor, smoke, and perspiration immediately brought her hand to her face in an effort to lessen the pungent odor. She looked at Jasmine, who did not seem to notice the smell at all.

Jasmine led Bess to the bar and got the attention of the tavern keeper. He was a surly, squat man, who did not appear the slightest bit surprised to see two girls of sixteen inside his tavern.

"What can I get you?" he asked gruffly.

"We're looking for someone and hoped you might be able to help us."

Jasmine thought the direct approach would be their best course of action, but immediately saw her mistake when the man turned to help one of his paying customers. As soon as she could get him to look their way again, she took out a coin and put in on the bar.

"Two ales, please."

The man looked mollified and poured them their ale.

As he placed the cups before the girls, he said, "Who you lookin' for?"

"That's the problem. We don't know his name," Jasmine began, then seeing his look of impatience, continued quickly, "but he's tall, with black hair and a short beard. He's expensively dressed, all in black, too. Have you seen someone like that?"

"Can't say that I have. Why are you lookin' for him?"

Jasmine hadn't anticipated that question and was at a loss to come up with a suitable excuse. She was surprised when Bess answered,

"We saw him in the marketplace today. He stole something from my father's shop. Rather than get the sheriff involved, I thought if we found him we could persuade him to return the item."

Jasmine saw the man look Bess up and down, as though trying to decide if he should believe her story.

"Well, I haven't seen him," he tersely responded as he turned away from them and went to the other end of the bar.

The girls quickly left the tavern, not bothering to finish their ale.

"That went well," Bess remarked sarcastically.

"We can't expect to find him on the first try," Jasmine replied. "There are many more taverns to visit, though. We cannot lose hope yet."

Bess agreed and they went on to search four more taverns, each with the same result. They were approaching Jasmine's street and came across the Black Ox. Jasmine sped up her pace, hoping Bess would not notice the tavern.

"Wait! There is another tavern, just to your right," Bess pointed out.

Jasmine did not need to look, instead turned to Bess and said, "It is getting rather late, perhaps we should continue the search tomorrow?"

"Nonsense. We are here, and we might as well inquire within. Then we can stop if you wish."

Jasmine knew she had no hope of evading the inevitable. She silently prayed that her father had already gone home and Bess would not see him in such a place. With enormous dread, she swung open the door and prepared herself for the worst.

What she saw next, however, she could not have anticipated and was instantly filled with embarrassment. She did not want to look at Bess for fear of what she might find in her expression.

Bess noticed Jasmine stiffen next to her and was about to ask her what was wrong when she saw the answer to her question. Jasmine's father was standing on a table at the back of the tavern, drink in hand, singing a bawdy song as loud as the church bells that chimed the time of day. He was so animated, focusing on singing his song with such earnestness that Bess could not hide her amusement, however hard she tried. She finally gave in to her impulse and laughed as she had not laughed for a long, long time.

Jasmine heard Bess' outburst and took another look at the scene in front of her. Now that she was no longer fearful of her friend's disgust, she could find the humor in it as well, and gave herself over to the contagious laughter.

When they had both calmed down, they decided it would be best if they did not attract the attention of Jasmine's father, and silently left the tavern.

"Let's come back tomorrow," Bess suggested and Jasmine was quick to agree.

The joviality of the last few moments had not died, and they found themselves making jokes and reliving the experience all over again. The girls were so wrapped up in their merriment that they did not notice the sound of footsteps behind them.

"What are you two up to?"

Both girls were startled and quickly turned in the direction of the voice.

"William!" Bess exclaimed. "You scared me!"

William came closer and said, "That is not an answer to my question, Bess. Whatever are you doing going into these taverns?"

"How long have you been following us?" Jasmine inquired.

William ignored her question and pulled Bess away, said in a softer tone, "This is no place for you. I'll take you home."

Bess did not like the commanding nature of his request and freed her arm from his grip.

"I was on my way home when you so rudely interrupted us. Jasmine and I are doing something very important; you need not interfere."

"When that 'something important' includes visiting taverns, I do need to interfere! Imagine what father would say!"

"If father knew why we are doing what we are doing, I am certain he would understand," Bess responded.

"He might understand, but he would never approve; you know that as well as I."

Jasmine had stood by and watched this exchange, now tried to intervene.

"It is my fault," she proclaimed. "I suggested this course of action to Bess. Perhaps it was not such a good idea."

William turned to face her.

"No, it certainly was not a good idea! If this is what comes of Bess' friendship with you, I would ask that you leave my sister alone!"

Jasmine was wounded by the tone in his voice and the look in his eyes. She turned and, fighting the desire to run, walked down the street toward her home with as much dignity as she could muster.

Bess looked at her brother as if she did not know him. What could have possessed him to act so shamelessly to her friend? Too angry for speech, she had not the same restraint as Jasmine and ran all the way to Cardwell Hall.

Bess heard a knock on her bedchamber door. Knowing it was William, she purposefully chose not to respond to it, instead pulled the velvet coverlets up higher about her chin.

She heard a faint, "Bess, please open the door. I need to speak with you!"

The emotion in her brother's voice softened her resolve, however, and she quickly rose from the bed and put on her dressing robe.

Unlatching the heavy door, she said, "I hope you are here to apologize, Will."

William stepped into the chamber and Bess shut the door behind him.

He slowly went to the small sideboard and poured himself a cup of wine, gathering his thoughts in order to explain to his sister why he had behaved the way that he had.

"I am sorry, Bess, if I have offended you or your friend. But you must understand that I only have your best interests at heart."

Bess sat on her coffer, an inscrutable expression on her face, waiting for her brother to continue as he paced from the sideboard to the window and back again.

"You are sixteen years old, dearest. You cannot stay a child forever, and your recent actions do not befit a girl of your station and age. Frequenting taverns might be an acceptable activity for your new friend Jasmine, but it is certainly not acceptable for you!"

Bess began to protest, but William stopped her, asked her to hear him out.

"I had hoped to avoid speaking of this, but the truth is that some of your friends are already betrothed, while you are cultivating a friendship with someone who can only serve to diminish your prospects."

William saw the shocked look on his sister's face, knew she had not entertained the possibility of marriage.

"But I do not even know of any potential suitors, Will! Surely I am going to have the opportunity of falling in love first!"

"That is a luxury few can afford where wealth and influence are concerned. Father has worked hard to make the Cardwell name mean something, even in the highest circles. What do you think he would say if he knew his sixteen year old daughter had been seen in a local alehouse?"

"At least he would then know that I am alive!" Bess responded quickly, rising from the coffer. "Honestly, Will, can you expect me to believe that he would care what I do? He barely acknowledges my existence, and if my conduct helps prevent an unwanted marriage, so much the better!"

William shook his head, knowing his words had fallen on deaf ears. He was not prepared, however, for what he would hear next.

"And I must tell you, William Cardwell, that you are quite the hypocrite! One day you are telling me that Jasmine has feelings and that God cares for her as much as He does for us, the next you are berating my friendship with her. What am I to believe? That

God loves her, but it is not proper that I should be seen with her?"

"It is not proper that you should be seen with her inside a tavern! Am I not making myself clear? If you choose to spend time with Jasmine, do so in suitable surroundings, for heaven's sake!"

Bess knew that if she was to make her brother understand the importance of her recent actions, she would have to confide in him and reveal the whole story behind the theft of her pouch. She moved to the window, sat on the seat below and motioned for William to join her.

"There is something I have not told you, Will. Jasmine and I feel that the theft of my pouch was not simply for monetary gain. Do you remember the sheriff telling us that the murdered thief had a torn bit of paper clutched in his hand?"

William nodded, eager to hear his sister's next words.

"What you do not know is that one of Jasmine's friends stumbled upon the dead man's body, and found beside it five pounds!"

Bess saw the surprised look on her brother's face and continued.

"We believe that the thief was paid money in exchange for the note and that he gained possession of the note by stealing my pouch."

"But how on earth would such a note find its way inside your pouch?" William asked.

"That is what we are trying to find out. We want to know who put it in there and why."

"And you expect to find this information inside a tavern?" William asked sarcastically.

"Actually, we do. On the day of the theft, Jasmine saw a strange man who was dressed all in black following me. She thought he was about to do me harm, but before he could make his move, the thief came forward and stole my pouch. This man in black then ran after the thief. We believe that if we uncover information about the man in black, we might find out why he was following me, which may tell us more about the note and the theft. I know it is a suspect theory, but it is the only thing we could think of doing."

William pondered this revelation and asked, "Why do you not simply inform the sheriff and let him look into this?"

"Because Jasmine does not wish to involve her friend, thinking he might be held accountable for taking the five pounds in the first place. She also believes he might be accused of the murder."

"And are you so sure that he is innocent?" William surprised her by asking.

"I had not thought about it, in truth. But I do believe Jasmine knows her friend well enough to vouch for him, and that is good enough for me."

Wanting to admonish Bess for her naivety, William rose from the window seat but said nothing, needing to digest these new facts.

Before he could speak, Bess pleaded, "Please Will, do not tell anyone of the things I have told you. Jasmine and I promised to keep this a secret until we can uncover more information.

"In truth, Bess, I do not know who I would tell. Few people would credit such a fantastic theory. There could be many other explanations for the extra money by the body and the piece of paper in the man's hand. With so little evidence, I wonder at your hope of ever finding out what really took place."

"I know we may never know the truth, but trying to discover it is ever so much fun! Attempting to unravel a mystery is far better than spending my days attempting to avoid Alice!"

At that, William could not resist letting a smile play upon his lips.

"I am glad that you have found a pleasurable activity, Bess, but please leave the taverns out of your plans from now on!"

As William looked at his sister, he found an excitement in her eyes that he had not seen in a very long time. He could not squash her enthusiasm, instead vowed that he would keep an eye on her in the future.

"There seems to be nothing left to say. I will bid you goodnight then, dearest. All I ask is that you keep me informed on your progress. You will do that, will you not?"

Bess rose from the window seat as one who had just been reprieved from the gaol and flew into her brother's arms. Kissing him on the cheek, she said, "How can I thank you for being such a dear?"

"Just be careful. That is all I ask."

The morning sky promised a bright and sunny, if not overly warm, October day. Generally on Saturdays Jasmine's father opened his shop in the morning and worked until noon or one o'clock. This Saturday, however, found Mr. Bowles' butcher shop tightly closed up, as it had been the day before.

Jasmine sat at the small table, trying to complete her embroidery, all the while wondering if her father would ever rise from bed this morning. He had come home late the night before, stumbling up the stairs, singing the same song that he had bellowed earlier that day inside the tavern. He had not gone on such a binge since Jasmine's mother had died, and she hoped that he would not repeat his actions of one year ago. It had taken him over a month to stop drinking that time, and Jasmine had found herself unable to mourn properly, needing instead to take in as much sewing work as possible to keep the family from starving.

She rose and heaped more coals upon the brazier, trying to banish the cold as well as her unsettling thoughts. She heard footsteps above her, and thanked God that her father had awoken at last. She fetched some fresh bread and cheese from the pantry, knowing he would be hungry. When she returned with the food, she found him already sitting at the table, pouring himself a cup of ale.

"Do you wish me to see Mrs. Stopplewick, get one of her special teas made just for mornings such as this?" she asked him cheerfully, hoping to conceal her worry.

"No thank you, my dear. I feel much better already," he replied, after taking a huge gulp of ale.

"Are you going to open shop today, Papa?"

"I believe I might do just that. What are your plans for the day?"

"I am going to complete this embroidery and take it to the baker's wife," she answered, not divulging her plans with Bess. She did not wish to be secretive, but also did not wish to lie to her father when the inevitable questions arose regarding their activities. It was best if he continued to be unaware of their investigation into the murder of the thief.

After Mr. Bowles had finished eating, he went downstairs to open his shop. Jasmine was able to complete her needlework just in time to keep her arranged meeting with Bess at the churchyard.

She was surprised to find that Bess had not arrived yet, and made her way to the familiar gravestone of her mother to wait for her friend. Touching the cold stone, she silently prayed for her father. She was still unsure whether his latest outburst of drinking would last overly long, wished there was something she could do to help him. She was so wrapped up in her thoughts that she didn't hear Bess approach.

"Jasmine?" Bess said quietly, not wanting to startle her friend. She had noticed that Jasmine's eyes were closed, knew she was praying, and hoped that the pain over the loss of her mother was not too hard to bear. Still, at least Jasmine had known her mother, had memories to hold on to and cherish.

"Hello," replied Jasmine, "are you ready for another day of inquiries?"

"I do need to speak with you about that," Bess began cautiously, hoping Jasmine wouldn't think her a snob for what she was about to say next. "I cannot enter the taverns with you today. I am sorry, but I have promised my brother William."

"I am sorry, too. I certainly did not wish for you to incur your brother's wrath because of me," Jasmine responded.

"Oh no! It is I who should apologize to you for William's behavior. His quarrel is not with you, however it may have seemed last night. He simply does not think it appropriate for me to be seen inside a tavern. I had to promise him that I would heed his wishes in this, or he might have gone to father and told him everything!"

"Everything?" inquired Jasmine.

Bess flushed, did not look Jasmine in the eyes as she spoke.

"I told him of our theory about the theft of my pouch. I did keep Harry's name out of it, I assure you! But he needed to know why we were visiting the taverns; truly, I had no choice but to tell him."

Bess saw Jasmine's look of apprehension and said quickly, "He promised not to tell another soul, and William always keeps his promises."

Jasmine thought for a moment. She knew that they could not keep this a secret forever and would have to come out with their findings, if indeed they did discover anything of interest, which certainly had not happened yet. Then she realized that it was not fear of William knowing what they were doing that distressed her, but fear that he would think them childish, pursuing this mystery as if they could actually solve it. At that moment she felt younger than her sixteen years, for the first time doubted her ability to uncover anything at all.

She said to her friend, "What's done is done, I suppose. Let's not dwell on it, shall we?" for which Bess looked grateful.

Bess linked her arm through Jasmine's as they walked out of the churchyard.

"I almost forgot," said Jasmine, stopping abruptly. "I need to take this embroidery to the baker's shop on Stonegate. Do you mind if we start there and work our way back to The Shambles?"

"Not at all," replied Bess, and they changed their course and travelled west until they reached the shop.

They entered the bakery and Jasmine handed the baker's wife the embroidered linens she had completed and received her payment in return.

Once they were outside the shop, Jasmine announced, "Looks as though I can pay for our dinner today! Perhaps later we can stop at the marketplace and purchase some meat pies?"

"I will not hear of you spending your hard-earned money on me, Jasmine Bowles! I receive a weekly allowance for doing nothing at all, so I shall pay for our dinner!"

Jasmine was about to protest, then remembered that her father had lost a day's earnings yesterday and thought better of it. He might not be pleased to hear that she had squandered some of her money.

Instead she smiled at Bess and said, "I know better than to argue when I have no chance of winning!"

That made Bess laugh. "If only I had the same sensibility! I would save myself some frustration, for certain!"

They continued on their way back to The Shambles, stopping at several taverns along the way. Bess made sure not to enter any of them, and Jasmine was quick to relate to her what had transpired inside each. Usually Jasmine received the same response, that no one had seen such a man. The latest tavern keeper she questioned, however, gave her a new answer.

"Aye, I've seen someone who fits that description," he surprised Jasmine by saying.

Her heart started to pound. "Can you tell me when you saw him?" she asked.

"Few days ago, I should say."

"Was he with anyone?"

"No. Just sat in the corner by himself, had a meal and some ale, and left soon after."

Jasmine was disheartened. Was that it? Was that the only information she and Bess would receive after all of their searching the past two days?

"Can you tell me anything else about him? What time did he come in?"

"It was well past Compline. Now that I think about it, he did seem a bit surly. The serving maid commented on his gruffness, said he was as angry as a hunter who had lost his prey. And if Lucy failed to put a smile on his face, he must have been angry indeed!"

This last comment was lost upon Jasmine, whose mind was trying to absorb this new information. She mumbled her thanks to the helpful tavern keeper and went outside to relate her story to Bess.

"He said that he came in a few days ago, after Compline. Wednesday night, perhaps? The same night the thief was murdered and Harry made off with the money?" Jasmine proposed excitedly.

"Do you suppose that the man in black was the murderer? It seems to fit the circumstances, does it not?" asked Bess. "He could have followed the thief, caught up with him that night in the stables, offered him the five pounds, then killed him to gain possession of the note. Harry scared the man in black off before he could gather the fallen money, and now he is after Harry for taking it."

Jasmine pondered that for a moment before answering, "That would explain his anger, to be sure. But if he gained possession of the note from the thief, I just don't think he would be bothering Harry about the money. The note seems to be the thing of importance here. It is more likely that he failed to procure the note, and is now trying to find out who has it. Thinking that it might be Harry, he ransacked his house looking for it, but to no avail."

"Are you sure it *was* to no avail? Would Harry tell you if he had the note? Would he even realize the significance of it? Perhaps the man in black did find the note in Harry's house, and we have seen the last of him," suggested Bess.

"The more we know about this, the more complicated it seems to get," complained Jasmine.

Both girls let out a long sigh, wondering if their investigation was coming to an end.

"I'm hungry," announced Jasmine. "Perhaps eating something will help stimulate our minds."

"Shall we go in search of those meat pies you suggested?"

Jasmine agreed with a smile and they made their way to the marketplace. After finding a vendor who sold meat pies, they sat on a nearby bench and ate them hungrily. Before they could finish, however, Harry came running up to them, breathless.

"Harry! You remember Bess, do you not?" asked Jasmine cheerily.

Harry cast a quick glance at Bess before exclaiming, "Jasmine, you'll never believe what just happened!"

"Sit down, Harry, catch your breath!" Jasmine instructed. She knew Harry was ever one for exaggerating, had probably almost gotten caught stealing again, nothing more serious than that.

After plopping down beside Jasmine, Harry took a few deep breaths and continued, "My very life was just threatened!"

This caught Jasmine off guard. "By whom?" she asked.

"I don't know. A man. Very tall, with black hair and beard, dressed all in black!"

Chapter Six

The two girls involuntarily stood up from the bench on which they were sitting. Harry did the same as he prepared for their questions. As much as he was frightened by what had happened to him, he enjoyed being the center of attention, and if he stretched the boundaries of the facts a little, so be it; he was entitled to their sympathy after what had just befallen him.

"What did the man in black say?" asked Jasmine, trying to comprehend the meaning of this.

"He said that he saw me go into the stables that night, and if I knew what was good for me, I'd tell him why."

Jasmine could not believe she hadn't thought to ask the same question, now looked at Harry and said, "Why did you go into the stables?"

"Tom and I were playing a game, that's all. I was simply trying to hide. If I had known I'd run into a dead body, I would have hidden somewhere else, to be sure!"

"Did you tell the man in black that?"

Harry nodded. "Then he asked me if I had taken anything from the stables."

"And what did you tell him?"

"I told him I took the money which was lying on the floor, but that I gave it back as soon as I found out who it belonged to," he told them, glancing at Bess. "But he wasn't satisfied with my answer, pushed me up against the wall of the alley so hard I thought he was going to break my neck!"

"Oh my!" Bess exclaimed, her eyes opening wide as her hand went to her mouth.

Harry took great pleasure in seeing her concern for his safety, but frowned when he saw only impatience in Jasmine's eyes.

"But he didn't break your neck, did he? What else did he say?" Jasmine inquired.

"He asked if I had seen anyone there that night, and when I told him no, he said that if he found out I was lying he would come after me, said he knew ways to force the truth from me!"

"And were you lying?"

"Jasmine! Do you really think I would have lied when my life was in jeopardy?"

"Honestly Harry, I don't know. Would you?"

Harry did his best to appear stricken by her words. Instead of answering, however, he changed the subject.

"I went by your house trying to find you, but no one was there. I'm certainly surprised to see the two of you together. How did that come about?"

"That's a long story, Harry, best saved for another time. Did you tell the sheriff about what happened?"

"No, of course not! Do you want me to end up in the gaol for taking the money in the first place?"

Bess had been a spectator up until this point, now tried to enter the conversation by saying, "I do not think that need happen. I can explain to the sheriff that the money was returned to me in due course. That will help, will it not?"

"Aye, except for the fact that I knew a crime had been committed, yet took the money anyway, instead of reporting it to the sheriff," explained Harry.

"I don't think we have much of a choice," Jasmine told him. "The man in black has searched your house, has now threatened you as well. It is time that we told the sheriff everything."

"Wait a moment. You think that it was this same man who ransacked my house?" asked Harry, who had not yet made that connection.

"Certainly that cannot be in doubt anymore?"

Bess nodded her head in agreement with Jasmine.

Harry was not about to concede however, and said, "Can we not go to the sheriff and tell him what happened without mentioning the fact that I took the money?"

"Thomas Wainwright already thinks that the killer stole the money from the thief, perhaps we can let him continue in his assumption?" offered Bess.

Harry smiled. At first he did not think much of this obviously wealthy girl, had put up with her presence for Jasmine's sake, but now found cause to re-evaluate his opinion. Perhaps he was too hasty in his dislike of Bess. Besides, if Jasmine had become friends with her, he supposed she could not be without some good qualities.

"Aye, let's let him think that, shall we?" he quickly added.

It was against her better judgment, but Jasmine found she could not go against her two friends, and she certainly did not want to get Harry into trouble if she could help it.

Harry knew that Jasmine's silence was a sign of her agreement, and he led the two girls in search of the sheriff.

They found Thomas Wainwright at the other end of the marketplace conversing with one of the merchants. They waited until he had completed his dialog before approaching. He was certainly surprised to see this group coming forward, and thought what an incongruous threesome they made. He could not help but wonder why a girl of Bess' upbringing should be casting in her lot with these two young commoners.

"Good day to you all," he said gallantly.

"Good day, sheriff."

It was Jasmine who spoke. She had been selected to relate their story to the sheriff, now felt uncertain of how to begin.

"What can I do for you?" asked Thomas.

"We wanted to tell you about something... someone, to be exact, who relates to both of the crimes against Harry and Bess," she began, unsure of whether or not the sheriff would even want to hear her information.

Thomas' interest was piqued, bade them to follow him to the clearing behind the marketplace.

His face was all business as he instructed, "Tell me what you know."

Jasmine started at the beginning, with her first glimpse of the man in black at the marketplace as he was following Bess. She then told him of seeing the man in black following Harry yesterday, and that this same man threatened Harry's life earlier this very morning.

Bess studied Thomas' face as Jasmine spoke, noticed the green eyes focused upon her as she related the tale. His thoughts were inscrutable; he betrayed neither belief nor disbelief at her words.

When Jasmine had finished speaking, Thomas looked at Harry, who had difficulty meeting his gaze.

"What did this man in black say to you, lad?" he asked.

"He asked me if I had seen anyone at the blacksmith's stables the night of the murder," Harry replied honestly.

"And did you?"

"No sir. Well, the dead body, of course."

"Of course. Do you think this was the same man who broke into your house yesterday morn?" Thomas questioned.

"I don't rightly know," Harry began, then looked at Jasmine and said, "We think so."

Thomas turned suddenly to Bess.

"Why have you been looking for this man?"

Bess was dumbfounded by his question. How did he know she and Jasmine had been looking for the man in black?

Jasmine had the same thought and shot back before Bess could answer, "How did you know we were looking for him, sheriff?"

"I make it a point to keep myself well-informed," he told her. "But you did not answer my question. Why are you looking for him?"

"We simply wish to gain information about him. Why was he following Bess? And what does he hope to gain by stalking Harry?" Jasmine answered.

"The most likely answer is that he was about to steal your friend's pouch, followed and murdered the real thief, took the money, and is now making sure that Harry did not see him at the scene of the crime. Does that not seem so?"

"That is certainly possible," agreed Jasmine non-commitally. She had no intention of revealing to the sheriff that the man in black did not take the money. She supposed that he could have murdered the thief and is now trying to cover his tracks, but then why ask Harry about what he took from the scene of the crime? Unless he did not gain possession of the note as Bess had suggested and is now looking for it.

"Are you going to try to find this man, sheriff?" Bess spoke for the first time and was heartened to see Thomas' face soften when he looked at her.

"I will certainly do my best, Miss," he responded.

She bowed her head slightly and said, "Thank you sir."

"I will be off then," Thomas announced, adding, "and please, leave the man hunt to me from now on!"

After having milled about the marketplace for the better part of an hour, Jasmine purchasing a head of cabbage to boil for supper and some more barley flour, the three friends decided to return to their homes. Before departing, Harry said goodbye to Bess, and asked Jasmine if he would see her tomorrow at church.

"I listen to one Vespers service with you and now you think that I shall attend regularly?" Jasmine asked him playfully.

"Of course! My mother said how glad she was to see you there and wanted me to invite you to come again, said she will save a place for you and your father," he informed her.

"Your mother is a sweet woman, but ever the voice of conviction. Did you know that she even suggested I tell my father about playing football?"

"You didn't, did you?" asked Harry, quite worried that the best person on his team would not be able to play anymore.

"What do you think? If my father found out, I'd be house-bound for a month!" Jasmine exclaimed.

Bess had listened to this exchange with interest, now waved goodbye to Harry as he took his leave. She did not know if she should brooch the subject with Jasmine, did not wish to offend her.

Curiosity won out over good manners, however, and she decided to ask, "Do you not attend church, Jasmine?"

Jasmine paused before answering. How much did she wish to reveal to Bess? She did not want to appear to be a heathen, but was that not how she had been acting lately?

"My family used to attend church regularly, before my mother died. We have not gone since then. You see, my mother was a very pious woman. She loved God with all her heart and wanted nothing more than to be inside the church, praying for her family, feeling close to God. My father, I believe, finds it too painful; I cannot be sure, but I think he blames God somehow for her death."

"And what about you?"

"As you heard Harry mention, I did go to Vespers with him on Thursday. Somehow, there is a great difference between going to the churchyard to visit my mother's grave and actually entering the church. Once inside, I found that the memories of my mother were almost too strong to bear; I had to fight back the tears. I felt better for having gone, though. I wish my father could do the same."

"Jasmine?" Bess began, hoping her question would not exceed the boundaries of rudeness. "Can you read and write?"

Jasmine smiled, answered readily, "Yes, I can. My mother taught me. She was an amazing woman, in truth. She was the daughter of a wealthy tradesman, married beneath her status when she married my father. Her family never forgave her, cut off all contact with her. I do not even know who my grandparents are, as a matter of fact. Needless to say, she was educated as any upper-class young woman would have been, and later she passed on her knowledge to me."

Bess was glad to hear that, had known there was something different about Jasmine once they had begun their friendship. She had a feeling that Jasmine was not like the other common girls, not that she knew any of them personally, of course, but somehow Bess felt a kinship to her, as though they were quite alike in many ways.

"I am wondering if I might give you my Book of Hours," Bess surprised herself by offering.

Tears immediately came to Jasmine's eyes. Bess could not help but see them and put her arm around her friend, saying, "I am so sorry. I did not mean to cause you hurt!"

"No. You don't understand," Jasmine responded, wiping her tears on the sleeve of her gown. "My mother always kept her Book of Hours with her, read from it throughout the day. She even read it to me at bedtime, and I would fall asleep to the sound of her voice. She had requested that the prayer book be buried with her and ever since, how I have longed for one of my own! I finally gave up hope once I realized that my father would never be able to afford to buy one."

"Well then, it is settled. You shall have mine," Bess told her.

Jasmine was too moved for speech, instead grabbed Bess' hand and held it tight. Perhaps she would go to church tomorrow; she had much to thank God for.

For the Cardwell family, supper consisted of roast pork, boiled mutton, cheese imported from France, manchet bread, and stewed apples. Bess' father could not join them this evening, was still at the guild hall preparing the King's share of the quarterly profits that would be sent to London, making sure that nothing would be found amiss.

King Edward's favor was very important to the city of York and to the town's merchants. Edward had deposed the previous king, Henry of Lancaster, and was quick to find fault with the city that had long been a Lancastrian stronghold. Henry's queen, Margaret of Anjou, however, would not give up hope of regaining the crown for her husband and, in the future, for her son as well. There were always rumors of Lancastrian uprisings, most probably backed by Margaret, but always coming from the north, from Yorkshire.

Bess knew that this was an important time for her father, knew that she would not see much of him in the near future. She wished that his business would soon be concluded and that they could go back to Cardwell Manor. As she sat at the table, playing with her food, she was forced to re-think her position. Did she really want to go back to the Manor? Her family had always celebrated Christmas there; she could not imagine doing so anywhere else. But she was loath to leave Jasmine. They were fast becoming good friends, and if she went back to the Manor, she might not see Jasmine again for a very long time.

She thought of the events of the past few days and how she had changed since their inception. She now had an interest in life, would find herself smiling for the simple reason that she was alive and no longer felt alone. She thought of Jasmine and their friendship, of Harry and his unique, if not overly honest, personality, and of the sheriff who had captured her attention. Her mind strayed to Thomas Wainwright more than she would like to admit, and her heart skipped a beat as she remembered how he had looked at her that afternoon.

"Do not play with your food, Elizabeth," scolded Alice from across the table.

"What is the reason behind that smile of yours, Bess?" teased William, ignoring Alice's remark.

Bess looked at her brother, trying to hide her embarrassment. "Nothing, Will! I was simply remembering something humorous that Jasmine said today, that is all."

"You saw that girl again today?" asked Alice.

Bess found her anger rising, did not hazard a response.

"Her name is Jasmine," William reminded Alice in a tone that served as a warning.

Alice ignored him, focusing on Bess as she said, "I think it is to your advantage that we will be going back to the Manor soon, where you can again mix with appropriate society."

William tried to prevent a certain argument, said cheerily, "Speaking of appropriate society, are the Heatherton's not having a feast to celebrate Jane's birthday soon?"

Bess had forgotten all about it, now wished that William had too. She had no desire to attend a feast in honor of a girl whose only desire was to spend her father's money. She knew the Heathertons were wealthy; their family was almost as prominent in society as hers, but how long they could continue to be so with Jane's expensive tastes was unknown.

"I had forgotten, Will. November first, is it not? What bad luck to be born on Hallowmas! I would almost feel sorry for her, except that she seems to think that all of the holiday revelries be for her alone!"

"I, for one, am not overly eager to go," revealed William, "Sir Charles always gets a certain gleam in his eye when he sees me with his daughter. Gives me the chills!"

"Perhaps we can miss it this year?" suggested Bess.

"Do not even think such a thing!" Alice was quick to interject. "It would be a terrible affront to Miss Heatherton if you did not attend her birthday feast! I will hear no more about it, and I want the two of you to be on your best behavior Tuesday."

Bess looked at William, who knew exactly what she was thinking, that Alice had certainly perfected the 'motherly' reprimand. To Bess' surprise, however, she did not feel anger at it, instead had to stifle a laugh.

The rest of the meal passed without speech, and Bess ate quickly, anxious to be alone in her bedchamber and take her Saturday evening bath. She excused herself and found that Maude had made ready the tub, was already bringing up the hot water.

Ever since she and Jasmine had questioned Maude about the missing pouch, Bess had noticed a certain coolness in Maude's attitude toward her. She still did not think Maude responsible for putting the note inside her pouch, but she could not be sure, in turn, could not dispel Maude's fears with false words of assurance.

"Will there be anything else, Miss?" asked Maude, once she had filled the tub.

"No," Bess told her, then seeing her worried face, added, "And thank you very much, Maude."

Maude smiled and exited the chamber, leaving Bess alone to enjoy her warm bath and think about the excitement of the past few days.

As Jasmine prepared the boiled cabbage and pork she and her father would eat for supper, her mind strayed to what had happened earlier that day. She felt a keen disappointment that she and Bess would no longer be looking into the mystery behind the theft of Bess' pink pouch. After telling the sheriff about the man in black, all she and Bess could do now was wait to see if Thomas Wainwright could find him and question him about what had transpired inside the blacksmith's stables. He seemed to believe that the man in black was responsible for the murder of the thief, and even though Jasmine did not necessarily agree, she was pragmatic enough to know that the matter now lay in his hands.

She thought of the Book of Hours now safely tucked away inside her coffer, and marveled that Bess had given her so precious a gift. She had thanked God for it many times since this afternoon, said another quick prayer of thanks now and resolved to go to church on the morrow. Should she ask her father to attend with her? She knew that it would be difficult for him, but also knew that it was the only way he would begin to heal.

Jasmine made ready the table, set out the food she had prepared and called to her father. He came hurriedly down the stairs, eagerly anticipating his meal.

"Ah, you're a fine girl, Jasmine," he said as he sat down opposite her at the table.

He was beginning to eat when Jasmine interrupted, "Papa, I'd like to say a prayer before we eat. We used to before …"

She couldn't finish her sentence, didn't need to. Her father knew what she was going to say, that they used to pray at every meal before her mother had died.

"Aye, lass. We can pray if you'd like."

Jasmine said a short prayer of thanks, smiled at her father when she was finished. He returned her smile, if only briefly, before once again beginning to eat.

"Papa?"

"What is it now, child?" he responded between mouthfuls.

"I'd like to attend church tomorrow."

"That sounds like a fine idea, you should go. Yes, a fine idea," he mumbled without meeting her eyes.

"Would you go with me, Papa?"

John Bowles looked at his daughter, saw the trepidation in her eyes, knew the question had been difficult for her to ask. He also knew that it was something he could not do, even for her.

"No," he answered plainly, for what else could he say? How could he tell his daughter that he had lost all faith when he had lost his wife?

They passed the rest of the meal in silence, each unspoken thought serving as another rung on the bridge they had built between them.

Ever since Alice had married her father, Bess had a strong dislike for Sunday mornings. The thought of being seen in church with that woman as her stepmother never failed to give rise to Bess' anger. To her surprise, however, she didn't feel such heated emotion this Sunday morning. She had awoken to a bright blue sky and a heart filled with anticipation. She found it difficult to pinpoint the source of her happiness, but she nevertheless thanked God for it as she prepared herself for church.

Peering into the hall from behind her bedchamber door, Bess looked in vain for Maude. What could be keeping her? She was always at her side promptly each morning to help her dress and to do her hair. Bess shut the door and began to comb her hair herself. Before she could make an attempt at pinning it up, however, Maude rushed in, apologizing profusely.

"Do not fret, Maude. I am not angered," Bess assured her.

Maude was shocked at the words, even more so when she looked in Bess' eyes and saw that she was speaking the truth. She picked up an ivory comb and began to arrange Bess' hair.

"I do want to explain, Miss. I was late, you see, because of Joan."

"Joan?" inquired Bess, amused at the thought of hearing what was certain to be an interesting excuse.

"Yes, Miss. Ever since Lady Alice dismissed her, I've had to do some of her duties. Well, this morning Lady Alice asked me to mend her stockings, then when I was finished with that, she told me to do her hair. I tried to tell her that you were waiting for me, but she didn't seem to care."

"Of that I have no doubt!" Bess replied good-naturedly.

"I do hope she replaces Joan soon!"

"Do you know why she was dismissed?"

"No Miss. I only know that ever since last Wednesday I've been plum worn out trying to serve two ladies at the same time!"

Bess smiled at her maid, now certain that she had nothing to do with putting the note inside her pouch.

Jasmine paused on her way down the stairs. Should she ask her father once more if he would accompany her to church? He had looked sad when she had said goodbye to him, and her heart felt a heaviness now as she tried to decide what to do. She took another step, and another, until she was at the foot of the stairs, finally giving up her mind's useless struggle. If he wanted to come to church, he would come on his own. She knew her father well enough to realize that no amount of asking would make him change his mind once it was set.

She took in the crisp, cool air and the brightness of the blue sky as she made her way to Holy Trinity Church. Her spirits were lifted and the lightness of her gait reflected her new outlook. As she turned the corner toward the church, she heard her name being called from across the street. She turned and, seeing the Stopplewicks, ran across the street to meet them.

"Jasmine, dear. Are you heading to church?" asked Mrs. Stopplewick.

She nodded. Mrs. Stopplewick smiled and linked her arm through Jasmine's as they continued on their way.

Noticing the beautiful clasp on her cloak, Jasmine remarked to Mrs. Stopplewick, "My, but that's a lovely clasp. Is it new?"

Mrs. Stopplewick fingered the clasp gingerly.

"Yes it is. I can't remember when I've had anything so fine. Though it's only brass, you know, not gold. Goodness me, as if that matters! It's as beautiful as if it were gold, and more precious, too, because my Harry gave it to me."

Jasmine gave Harry a sidelong glance and he acknowledged her with a sly smile. She hoped he hadn't stolen the clasp. She knew that his mother had no idea of his penchant for thievery. Not that he had ever stolen anything of consequence. He was more interested in the act itself than of the gains. He seemed to enjoy the sport of it, and Jasmine had no doubt that Harry would soon tire of this recreation, just as he had all of his other hobbies.

They entered the stone church and Jasmine experienced the same feeling of nostalgia as she viewed her surroundings. They sat down only a few moments before the service began. Jasmine enjoyed the singing, listened with rapt attention to the sermon, and when the morning was over, she felt as though her life had returned to a level of normality that she never would have thought possible a year ago.

After saying goodbye to the Stopplewicks, she made her way home, stopping only to speak briefly with a neighbor before entering her house.

As she climbed the stairs, her father called down to her, "Jasmine, is that you?"

"Of course it's me, Papa. Who else would it be?" she responded cheerfully, before looking at her father's face. Seeing the slight apprehension in his expression, she suddenly became worried.

"What happened, Papa?"

"Oh, nothing really. A man came in the house unannounced, that's all."

Jasmine froze.

"What man?"

"Didn't give his name, but he left this for you," he answered, handing a note to his daughter.

Jasmine slowly unfolded the piece of paper and read its contents:

YOU ARE LOOKING FOR THE WRONG MAN.
MEET ME IN THE FOREST OF GALTRES
ON ALL-HALLOW'S EVE.
BEFORE THE BELLS RING COMPLINE
YOU WILL HAVE THE ANSWERS YOU SEEK.

Chapter Seven

Bess was eager to see Jasmine, wanted to go to the Shambles to relate the new information she had gathered from her maid. She was surprised, therefore, when she saw Jasmine being ushered into the solar by Alice, and went immediately to speak with her friend.

"Jasmine?" she inquired as she opened the solar door.

Alice was quick to answer in Jasmine's stead. "I was just getting acquainted with your new friend. Unfortunately, you did not give me much time to speak with her."

You mean interrogate her, do you not? Bess mutely retorted.

Ignoring Alice, Bess went to Jasmine and bade her sit with her on the window seat.

Alice seemed content to stay within earshot of their conversation, so Bess asked quietly, "Why have you come, Jasmine?"

Jasmine decided she could best answer her question by saying nothing at all, handed Bess the note she had received that morning.

Bess slowly opened the piece of paper and read its contents. Without saying a word, she grabbed Jasmine's hand and led her from the solar out to the gardens.

Once they were far enough from the house that no one could overhear their conversation, Bess quickly stopped.

"Who gave you this?" she asked.

Jasmine shook her head and replied, "I don't know for certain, but from my father's description, it must have been the man in black."

Bess' heart beat faster and her eyes flew open wide.

"You did not see him, then?"

"No. I was attending church. My father said that he came into the house without knocking and asked him to give the note to me upon my return."

"So he knew you were not there. He must have been observing your house and saw you leave," Bess surmised.

Jasmine nodded. The feeling of being watched had not left her since this morning, and she no longer felt secure walking the streets of the city alone.

"What did your father say?" asked Bess.

"What could he say? He thought it strange that a man should be entering his house with a note for me, of course. But I quickly explained it to his satisfaction."

"What could you possibly say that would ease his mind?"

"I told him that I was making a cloak for the man and that he had written down his instructions and measurements."

"And he believed you?" Bess asked incredulously.

"Apparently so," Jasmine responded.

"But how can you be sure he did not read the note before he gave it to you?"

"My father cannot read, so there is no risk of that."

That thought had not occurred to Bess, and she silently reproached herself for not being more sensitive.

"The strange thing," Jasmine continued, "is that the man in black must have known that I could read!"

Bess felt a now familiar tingle run up and down her spine as she thought about this fact.

"We must take the note to the sheriff," she instructed.

"Not until after All-Hallow's Eve."

"Jasmine, you are not going to meet with this man!"

"I must. Do you not see? He is the only one who can provide an answer to this mystery, and he will certainly not wish to speak in front of the sheriff. I have no choice but to meet him."

"Then I will accompany you," Bess told her.

"No, Bess. The note was given to me. I would not have you risk anything on my behalf."

"I would be risking far more by letting you go alone."

Jasmine was touched by Bess' remark, and once again marveled at the fact that they had become such good friends. Beginning to walk again, she knew she had no choice but to let Bess go with her. In truth, she would be glad for the company, for she had no desire to venture into the forest of Galtres alone.

Bess had to walk quickly to keep up with Jasmine, and as she quickened her pace, she remembered what Maude had told her that morning.

"Jasmine! I almost forgot to tell you!"

Jasmine slowed and asked, "Tell me what?"

"One of our servants was dismissed recently. She could have been the person who put the note inside my pouch!"

"Goodness! Why was she dismissed?"

"I do not know. That is a question only Alice can answer. Shall we go and ask her?" Bess suggested excitedly.

"By all means. I would be eager to hear what she has to say."

Jasmine and Bess found Alice sitting alone in the solar, working on a piece of embroidery for little Margaret.

Noticing their quick return, Alice commented, "Back as quickly as you departed, I see. And from the look on your faces, you require something of me."

"We do indeed, Madame," answered Jasmine.

"I have not seen Joan lately. Did you dismiss her?" asked Bess.

Alice's face immediately grew animated, mirroring her strong emotions regarding the subject.

"Yes, I certainly did. That girl was never where she was supposed to be. Did you know that I saw her speaking with a particularly shady character one evening in the courtyard when she was supposed to have been preparing my bath. And then when I found her rummaging through your father's antechamber...well, that was enough for me. I dismissed her the following morning."

"What day was that?" asked Jasmine.

"Wednesday last, I believe," Alice answered, her pose reflecting the recounting of a memory which had been buried beneath far more important matters.

Jasmine and Bess exchanged a knowing glance, each now sure of Joan's guilt.

"Thank you very much, Alice," said Bess, her face alight with excitement.

Alice watched as Bess and Jasmine hurriedly exited the solar, wondering at their strange behavior. Counting it as simple adolescent curiosity, she contentedly went back to her embroidery and thought no more about the incident.

Once inside Bess' bedchamber, the girls threw themselves upon the bed, reveling in their newfound discovery.

"Do you know what this means?" asked Jasmine, clutching a crimson velvet pillow.

"That Joan met with a strange man shortly before she went through my father's antechamber, and put the note inside my pouch," Bess was quick to answer. "Possibly the man in black?"

"Or it could have been the thief," suggested Jasmine. "Perhaps she told him that the information she was trying to obtain would be inside your pouch when you went to the marketplace."

"But how is the man in black involved, then?"

"That is what we must find out tomorrow night!"

Bess sighed. Everything always seemed to come back to the man in black.

Jasmine continued her thought regarding their conversation with Alice and said to Bess, "Alice said that Joan rummaged through your father's antechamber. What does he keep in that room?"

"He uses it to conduct business when he is not at the Guild Hall, so I would imagine he keeps business papers and such inside."

"Which means that Joan was searching for something that must have been pertaining to your father's business. So it is highly likely that the note contained whatever secret information she found."

Bess' excitement now turned to worry and fear. The guild meant a great deal to her father. What if his business affairs were now compromised? She must do something to help!

"Jasmine! We must find out what was on that note!"

"And we need to know who has the note now," added Jasmine.

Bess nodded her head vigorously, as if sheer will would somehow help them in their search. "We need to find Joan," she stated simply.

The remaining hours of Sunday, the thirtieth of October passed without incident. Bess and Jasmine had agreed to meet the following morning at Cardwell Hall to begin their search for the absent Joan. Bess now lay on her feather-filled mattress, trying to fall asleep, knowing she would not. Her mind was busy re-living the past few days, her heart pounding incessantly in anticipation of tomorrow. What would they discover about Joan and her activities? More worrisome, however, was the thought of meeting the man in black in the forest of Galtres. That is was dangerous, she already knew. That it would be helpful in solving the mystery, she had no doubt.

If only Jasmine would consent to telling the sheriff about the meeting! She knew that if he were present, no evil could befall them. But perhaps she only wished to tell the sheriff so that she could see him again! It seemed to Bess that all of her intentions were suspect when they involved Thomas Wainwright.

Rolling over onto her back, she pushed the coverlets down with her feet, freeing herself from their heaviness. Knowing that sleep would remain elusive, she decided to take a walk, hoping the activity would free her mind of its constant wanderings, and tire her body in the process.

Bess put her cloak on over her creamy-white silken dressing robe and ventured out of her bedchamber. The hallway was dark, the only light coming from a fading torch in the sconce on the wall, and as she held up her candle, she could discern the faint sound of wind as it pounded against the stone walls of her home. Proceeding down the hallway, she passed the other family bedchambers, finally coming to a circular stairway that led to the upstairs chambers of the servants. Climbing further up the staircase, she came to a small room that led out to the rooftop landing where she often came to sit and think. On a clear day she could see far off into the Yorkshire countryside, and Bess occasionally believed she could even see Cardwell Manor.

On this cloudy night, however, her view was greatly diminished; she could only hear the River Foss below as it ran south to meet the River Ouse. She walked to the other side of the landing, could now see more clearly due to the light of the lanterns that lit the courtyard. She set her candle down, letting the half-wall shield it from the wind, and leaned against the cold stone as the breeze played through her hair.

Her thoughts were interrupted by a low, shuffling noise. She strained to see where the sound had originated, moved along the wall in order to get a clearer view. She looked toward the courtyard gate and thought she saw a shadow lurking near the stone facade. Bess stood very still, hoping the shadow would move, or that she would again hear the foreign sound. Instead, her body began to ache from the cold and she longed to be inside her warm bedchamber.

I must have imagined it, Bess said to herself as she backed slowly away from the ledge. She was about to turn toward the door when she saw him; a shadowy figure that ran quickly past the gate and was lost behind the courtyard wall. Her eyes searched for him to no avail; she could only hear the sound of his shoes beating the stone path as he made his hasty retreat.

Jasmine hurried on her way to Cardwell Hall, not only because she was anxious to begin their search for Joan, but also because she had the feeling that the man in black could be anywhere, anytime, watching her movements. How else to explain his giving the note to her father when she was conveniently out of the house? The thought was unsettling, to be sure, and she was glad to be in sight of Bess' grand home.

She found her friend in the solar, working on a piece of embroidery.

"I am so glad you have come," Bess exclaimed as she rose from the settle, quickly discarding the embroidery. "You will not believe what I saw last night!"

"What?" Jasmine anxiously replied.

Bess told her of the man she had seen hovering around the courtyard gate.

"You didn't see his face?" Jasmine asked.

"No," said Bess, shaking her head. "He was in the shadow of the courtyard wall."

"Are you certain that it was a man?"

Bess' face showed her surprise at this question, and as she pondered it she realized she couldn't say for sure that it was a man.

"I suppose it could have been a woman," she offered hesitantly. "You do not think it was the man in black?"

"Although I am more than willing to blame him for almost any treacherous deed we can imagine, it might be folly to do so."

"I suppose you are right. But speaking of the man in black, are you still set on meeting him in the forest without the sheriff's knowledge?"

Jasmine pursed her lips together and nodded resolutely.

"Well then, I think we had better begin our search for Joan," Bess stated.

Jasmine agreed. "Where do we start?"

"I have already asked Maude if she knows where Joan is, but she said that she was not particularly close to Joan, had no desire to be, in truth."

"That would seem wise. Who else might know Joan's whereabouts?"

"I recall seeing her with the serving maid, Mary, from time to time. She should be in the kitchen."

"Lead the way, my Lady," Jasmine said playfully.

Bess took her through the great hall and into the now familiar kitchen.

Spotting Mary chopping herbs which would be used for their dinner, Bess motioned for her to join them in a secluded corner.

Mary looked at them expectantly. Can I be of help, Miss?" she asked Bess.

"Yes, Mary, we hope you may. You are friends with Joan, are you not?"

"Yes, Miss," she replied demurely.

"Do you know where she is?"

Mary looked confused. "Do you mean right now?"

"Has she found another post?" Jasmine quickly asked, hoping to clarify things for the maid.

"Aye, she has, and a right fine one, too," Mary was glad to answer.

After an expectant pause, Jasmine was forced to ask, "And where might this be?"

"She's in the service of Sir Charles Heatherton."

Jasmine noticed the startled look on Bess' face but continued her questioning by asking Mary if she knew why Joan had been rummaging through Bess' father's antechamber before being dismissed.

"I've no idea!" Mary exclaimed.

"You will not be in trouble, I assure you," Bess said. "But if you do know anything about the incident, please tell us."

"I wouldn't lie to you, Miss. I don't know a thing."

"Very well. You may go back to your work," Bess told her, disappointment showing on her pretty face.

After returning to the solar, Jasmine and Bess took a seat on the settle.

"You were surprised to hear that Joan is in the service of Sir Charles Heatherton?" Jasmine asked.

"My goodness, yes!" Bess exclaimed. "I cannot imagine that Alice gave Joan any kind of recommendation, and finding a post in such a distinguished household without one is almost unheard of."

"What is that saying," Jasmine began, "she has the 'Devil's own luck'?"

"I suppose so," Bess replied, still unable to explain such an occurrence. "But the good news is that William and I will be attending Jane Heatherton's birthday feast tomorrow, and I can try to speak to Joan then about her activities."

Jasmine tried to hide her disappointment that she would not be able to assist her friend in questioning Joan. She had the feeling her forcefulness of character might be needed to produce a response from the maid.

She carefully brooched the subject by asking, "Would it help if we went over what you are going to say to Joan in advance?"

Bess nodded vigorously. "Yes, please."

Jasmine was struck by Bess' humility, once again marveled that she had ever thought Bess a snob.

"Very well. We need to know why she was going through your father's business papers."

"I can certainly remember to ask that," Bess said.

"Yes, but you need to ask it in such a way that will make it difficult for her to refuse to answer," Jasmine instructed.

Bess looked unsure of Jasmine's meaning and responded with a simple, "How?"

"Make it clear to Joan that if she does not reveal the motivation behind her actions, then you will go to Sir Charles and tell him of the whole affair. She surely will think twice before jeopardizing another desirable post."

Bess burst into a smile, knowing that Jasmine's idea would guarantee success.

Jasmine busied herself by making a hearty stew for supper. She had already accomplished her work for the day by mending a cloak for the fishmonger and completing some embroidery for Matilda the brewer.

The sun was now setting fast and each new shade of darkness brought another knot to her stomach. October 31st, All Hallow's Eve; that the man in black would choose this night to meet in the forest of Galtres made her all the more apprehensive. She was thankful that Bess had not changed her mind about accompanying her, would not have blamed her if she had. They had agreed to meet after the church bells rang Vespers at six o'clock, which meant they would have three hours before the bells rang Compline; three hours in which to meet with the man in black and return before the city gates would close until morning.

So deep in thought was Jasmine that she didn't hear her father's approach.

"What a fine looking stew," Mr. Bowles exclaimed, patting his daughter on the shoulder.

Jasmine's heart leaped, as did the rest of her body.

"Didn't mean to startle you, lass!" he said with a little laugh. "Your mind must have been far away, yes, far away indeed."

She nodded at him sheepishly.

Jasmine had told her father she was meeting Harry for Vespers and then going home with the Stopplewicks to play draughts and taste Mrs. Stopplewick's famous apple tarts. She felt a twinge of guilt, therefore, looking at him now. She tried to push the thought away; how could she tell her father she was meeting a strange, perhaps dangerous, man in the forest that night? The thought occurred to her that if she couldn't tell him, perhaps she shouldn't be going. But again she chose not to listen to her sensible side and focused on the reasons she had to meet with the man in black, including making sure Harry was no longer in danger from him.

"Go sit down at the table, Papa; I'll bring in the stew and bread in a moment."

Mr. Bowles returned to the front room, leaving Jasmine alone to think upon her actions and try to justify her lie.

Bess had arranged for one of the grooms to take her to Jasmine's home shortly before Vespers. That afternoon at dinner, she had told her family she would be hearing Vespers with Jasmine and then returning to her home for supper. Alice was not overly pleased with this idea, but after her father had given his absent-minded consent, no one dared challenge his judgment. She had considered taking William into her confidence by telling him what they were planning to do, but knew he would never consent to such action and would either bar her from going or insist upon meeting the man in black with them. Now, as she entered the open carriage that would carry her to her friend's house, she secretly wished she had told William, even if it meant angering Jasmine.

The groom drove carefully in the darkness through the narrow streets of York until reaching their destination. Asking him to return at Compline, Bess descended from the carriage and stood facing the butcher's home. She had agreed to meet Jasmine at Holy Trinity Church and, with lantern in hand, made her way there as quickly as possible.

She approached the grassy churchyard just as the bells began to ring. As the other parishioners were hurriedly filing into the church, Bess walked instead to the tombstone of Jasmine's mother. She found her friend kneeling beside it, knew Jasmine to be in prayer, and hoped she was impeaching God to watch over them this evening.

Hearing footsteps behind her, Jasmine turned her head and saw Bess. Smiling, she said, "Are you certain you wish to do this?"

"No," Bess replied, returning her smile.

"Let's be off, then," Jasmine said, rising from her knees.

They made their way through the maze of gravestones until they left the churchyard and came to a street named Petergate, which would take them through Bootham Bar, the city gate to the north. Even though the moon was round and bright, they held their lanterns up high to further light their way. Jasmine was about to ask Bess what she had said to make her escape from her family this evening, when all of a sudden she felt a hand grip her shoulder.

Spinning around, she saw that it was only Harry.

"Harry, you rogue! You gave me a fright!" Jasmine exclaimed, slapping him on the chest for emphasis.

"My apologies, ladies," he said, with a mischievous grin on his face.

"What are you doing here?" Jasmine asked.

"Following you," he replied.

"That much is obvious. Why are you following us?"

"I saw you both leave the churchyard, knew whatever you were up to would be much more fun than attending Vespers. What *are* you up to, anyway?"

"That is none of your business! Now be off with you before I..."

"Before you what?" he challenged before Jasmine could finish.

Jasmine looked at Bess helplessly.

"I suppose we may as well tell him," Bess said, secretly hoping he might prevent them from going into the forest.

"Very well. But you must promise not to tell another soul," Jasmine warned.

"I promise," Harry replied eagerly.

"We are going into the forest to meet the man in black."

Harry's face showed his astonishment.

"Are you insane? He nearly killed me and yet you decide to go into the forest alone to meet him? I took you for a girl with more sense than that, Jasmine. And you," he continued, looking at Bess, "What could possess you to go along with such a scheme?"

"Jasmine was set upon going. I could not let her go alone, nor could I betray her trust by revealing what she planned to do," she stated simply.

Harry ran his fingers through his red hair, shook his head and announced, "Then I am coming with you."

This was not the result Bess had hoped for, but it was far better than she and Jasmine traveling into the forest alone.

Jasmine had other feelings about the matter, however, and said, "The man in black asked to meet me in the forest, not you. What if your presence angers him all the more?"

"We'll have to take that risk; or perhaps you wish me to tell your father where you are going?"

Jasmine responded by rolling her eyes and continuing down the street, allowing herself a little smile as she heard both sets of footsteps following her. In truth, the closer she got to the city gate, the more apprehensive she became, and she couldn't help but be slightly relieved to have Harry accompany them.

They continued to walk briskly until they were within sight of Bootham Bar, when their pace slowed considerably, each with a unique reason for hesitating. Jasmine was worried because she had Bess and Harry with her and didn't know how the man in black would react. Bess didn't think they should be going in the first place and now felt an emotion quite unfamiliar to her: fear. Harry was grappling with feelings of inadequacy, hoping it would not be necessary to protect the girls with a bravery he did not possess.

Entering the rounded passageway of the stone gatehouse, Harry said aloud what they were all thinking, "It's not too late to turn back."

No one responded to his reminder, but continued walking until they were within sight of the wall of trees that marked the beginning of the forest of Galtres.

"Should we enter?" Bess asked with trepidation.

"The note said to meet him *in* the forest, did it not?" Jasmine replied.

Holding her lantern high, she led her friends through the outer cusp of trees, proceeding deeper into the forest until they could no longer see the city walls. The moon's glow which had helped light their way was now obstructed by the high canopy of fir branches above them.

Bess felt extremely small among such an expanse of trees. She had ridden through the forest many times, but had always been with a large retinue of family and servants, and had always traveled during daylight hours.

"Surely we can stop? We *are* in the forest now, and I am certain the man in black will have no problem finding us if he wishes to."

"I agree with Bess," Harry said eagerly.

"I don't think..."

Jasmine's words were interrupted by the sound of horse's hooves. A rider was fast approaching from behind.

They turned with a start, staring at the hooded figure racing toward them. As he pulled in reign just a few feet before them, Jasmine felt her body grow tense, anticipating the cold grey eyes of the man in black. Would he be wroth to see that she had allowed her friends to accompany her?

The rider turned his face toward them and ripped back his hood.

"William!" Bess shouted.

Jasmine heaved a sigh of relief. Until that moment, she had not comprehended the extent of her fear at meeting the man in black. She couldn't help but let a little smile slip as she watched William descend from his horse.

Bess, however, had no smile to give her brother. "I cannot believe you followed me!" she accused.

"And I cannot believe you would be so foolhardy as to venture out into the forest alone," her brother retorted.

Bess looked at Jasmine and Harry and said, "As you can see, I am not alone, and I am fully capable of looking after myself."

Ignoring her remark, William turned his attention to Jasmine. "What are you doing here in the forest at this hour?"

Jasmine found that she had no words to offer.

William continued as if he did not expect a response, "I have had enough of you endangering my sister with your schemes!"

"Careful now," Harry interrupted. "You'd better watch how you speak to her, if you know what's good for you!"

William took a step toward Harry and said, "And what are you planning to do..."

Suddenly a voice came from behind them.

"If you wouldn't mind suspending your argument for a moment, I believe I have an appointment with this young lady."

Jasmine spun around to see the man in black's eyes focused upon her.

The group instantly fell silent, as if afraid to speak, or even to move.

"I see that I have caught you unawares. You are here to meet me, are you not?"

Jasmine swallowed hard, found that she could only nod her head.

"I do not recall asking you to invite guests," he continued, looking specifically at Harry. "Perhaps you felt the need of protection?"

Jasmine's mind raced to think of an answer. How could she respond to such a question? "You have done nothing to instill trust, sir," she finally said.

"Very true. But since we are all here and, it seems, in such a jovial mood," he said sarcastically, "allow me to ask why you have been looking for me?"

Jasmine could see that he was not a man who would be easily fooled, so she answered as honestly as possible.

"On the day that Bess' pouch was stolen in the marketplace, I saw you following her. After the thief took the pouch, you ran after him. Why?"

Jasmine saw his face show a moment's surprise at her answer, but he quickly recovered his cold countenance.

"I was merely trying to aid a young lady in the recovery of her pouch," he smoothly replied. "Did you think that I wanted the pouch for myself? As you can see, I am in no need of money."

Jasmine saw the fine horse that stood grazing a few feet behind him, saw the expensive cut of his clothes, the fashionable pointy shoes. She had to admit he did not look like an ordinary thief.

"And did you overtake the man who stole the pouch? Or did your fancy apparel prevent you from successful pursuit?"

A faint smile crossed his lips. "Alas, I could not find him once he had traversed the maze of the marketplace."

"But then you just happened to stumble across him at the blacksmith's stables that night?"

"I do not know what you mean."

"You threatened Harry because you knew that he had been there that night. If I am not mistaken, that means you must have been there, too," Jasmine accused.

The man in black looked slowly over the group, his eyes resting on Harry.

"I think your questions would be better directed at your friend here, rather than at me. He appeared to have a front row seat at the proceedings in the barn, and yet he tells me he saw nothing."

The man in black quickly mounted his horse, then said to Jasmine, "I came here tonight to tell you something. Now I will give you a warning. Stop trying to find me, stop looking into the murder. Nothing good can come of it, I do assure you."

Jasmine had never liked being told what to do, and coming from this man, it was even more distasteful.

Before he could make his exit, she shot back, "I believe you owe Harry an apology for ransacking his house."

Bess looked at Jasmine with wide eyes and her mouth slightly open, as if not believing what she had just heard. Harry quickly scanned the area, searching for a quick escape. William looked at Jasmine with a newfound appreciation and wondered to himself whether he would have had the courage to say the same thing.

The man in black, however, fixed his steel eyes on Jasmine while edging his horse as close to her as possible, and said to her alone, "Young lady, I apologize to none save God and the King, and not necessarily in that order."

He then spun around and spurred his horse forward, disappearing into the blackness of the forest.

"Jasmine!" Bess exclaimed. "How could you say such a thing? You have more nerve than even I gave you credit for!"

After watching the man in black ride away, Jasmine now turned to her friends with a blank look on her face, as if not believing herself what had just happened.

"What did he say to you?" Harry asked.

"Nothing," Jasmine murmured absently, as she began walking on the path they had taken that would lead them out of the forest.

"It wasn't about me, was it?" he continued. "Because if it was, you can tell him that I'm done with stealing, as you well know." He had to hurry to keep up with her, but still managed to ask, "He didn't threaten me again, did he?"

"No, Harry, he didn't threaten you again!" Jasmine replied, rolling her eyes. "I am quite certain it is me that he is not pleased with."

Harry couldn't help but breathe a sigh of relief, wishing now that he had stayed to hear Vespers with his parents.

William had been walking his horse behind them and now spoke up. "This was a foolhardy thing to do; I hope that has been made clear?"

Jasmine found herself agreeing with Bess' brother. They didn't gain any information from the man in black; in truth, it was he who had benefitted from their exchange by finding out why they had been searching for him. She and Bess still had as many questions as before.

William did not wait for an answer, instead mounted his horse and offered his hand to Bess, saying, "Come. I will take you home."

Bess took his hand and was soon riding toward the city gates. She turned to look back at Jasmine and mouthed a silent, "I am sorry" before the horse broke into a gallop.

Chapter Eight

The next morning found Bess preparing herself for Jane Heatherton's birthday feast. She had taken a nice warm bath, uncharacteristic for a Tuesday, using expensive French oils that her father had purchased for her on his latest visit to France. She now sat in front of her pier glass and pondered her reflection. Her azure gown with its long, full sleeves was becoming to her flawless complexion and enhanced the brightness of her blue eyes. Maude had dressed her blonde hair, brushing it until it shone, and was now preparing her veil and wimple. Bess was not overly fond of wearing a headdress, although she had no choice in the matter today as she could not offend the Heathertons by wearing anything but the fanciest and latest fashion.

She propped her head in her hands, gazed into the glass, and wondered if there was any chance that she might see Thomas Wainwright; or, more honestly, that he might see her. She was certain he would like what he saw.

Maude burst upon her reverie, however, by imploring, "Please Miss, sit up straight while I put on your wimple!"

Bess did as she bade, trying to sit as still as possible, while her mind took another turn. How would she manage to catch Joan alone so that she might question her about her activities? A flood of worry overcame her as she thought of the importance of her task.

Joan had been seen rummaging through her father's papers, and talking to an unsavory character late at night. Was it possible that she was in possession of one of her father's business secrets? Did the note in her pouch contain that information, and had the thief been killed in order to obtain it? But by whom? The man in black, or someone else entirely? She said a silent prayer, asking God to help her gain the information she sought; information that might be crucial to her family's future.

"All finished, Miss," Maude announced, quite pleased with the job she had done. "You look a picture, you do!"

"Thank you, Maude," Bess replied, sounding as cool as possible with her thoughts in such turmoil. "You have done an excellent job. I must be off now, but do not worry; I will tell you all about the festivities when I return."

"Godspeed, Miss," Maude said, "and have a fine time!"

Bess found William waiting for her in the great hall. She knew he was still upset with her after last night's episode in the forest, could see the agitated look in his face clearly.

"Hurry up, Bess, we do not want to be late!" he scolded her.

Bess followed her brother as quickly as possible although his long legs provided him with an advantage that her height could not afford. Once safely settled in the carriage, however, they were soon on their way to the Heatherton estate, just a short distance from the city.

Conversation between the two siblings was limited to observations about the weather and polite compliments on attire. Bess wished that she could somehow make amends with her brother, but she had already apologized on their way home last night; how many times would it take to make things right between them?

They reached their destination in due course and Bess alighted from the carriage with as much good humor as she could muster. She noticed that William did the same and was immediately seized upon by a long-time friend, leaving her to enter the great house alone. Why did she feel such trepidation? Surely she would be acquainted with all the other girls in attendance upon Jane. In truth, she had known most of them since she was a child and certainly had no reason for anxiety.

One of the servants opened the massive wooden door as she approached and bade her enter. She was then escorted to the great hall, where an unexpectedly large crowd was gathered, with little groups talking and laughing amongst themselves.

Luckily, she spied her childhood friend Mary among the throng of people and made her way toward her.

"Bess Cardwell!" Mary exclaimed, moving carefully through the crowd to keep from spilling her wine. "It is certainly good to see you! You have been far too long in York."

Mary's home was quite near Cardwell Manor, yet it was further from the city, and Bess had seen Mary only once this past summer.

"I admit it has been a long time," she replied. "My father's business in York is very pressing at the moment."

"Well then, I shall hope that all goes well and you are safely ensconced inside your beautiful Manor soon. Certainly before Christmas?"

"My father has promised, so I can guarantee you of that," Bess replied, as her eyes searched the room, hoping to find Joan serving wine among the guests. "And where might our hostess be?"

"Jane has taken a few intimates to her bedchamber to show them the satin material for her bridal gown," Mary informed her.

Bess was immediately shaken from her preoccupation with Joan and stared at her friend. "Her what?"

"Did you not hear? She has become betrothed to John Coggeshall of Essex. It is to be officially announced at the end of the feast, but I am certain that everyone here knows it," she answered, then sheepishly added, "Well, except you, it seems."

Bess had heard her father mention the Coggeshalls of Essex before, had gathered that they were one of the most powerful wool merchants in southeast England. This was certainly a coup for Sir Charles, but what about Jane?

"Is she in love with him?" she asked Mary, who immediately began to laugh.

"I did not remember you being so naïve, dearest. But I do hear that she is quite taken with him, although he is more than twice her age."

Now it was Bess' turn to laugh.

"Then I hope I shall never share her fate, but I wish her luck, nonetheless. I do hope they are as wealthy as they appear, however, for with Jane eyeing the purse strings, they shall certainly need to be!"

Mary put her hand to her mouth as if trying to stifle a giggle.

"Is the bridegroom in attendance?"

"Alas, no. He could not be spared from pressing business in London, it seems. I would not be surprised if you and I did not get a glimpse of him until the wedding," Mary predicted.

"And when is that to..." Bess' voice trailed off as she spotted Joan out of the corner of her eye. She was at the sideboard replacing the spent wine flagons.

"Please forgive me, Mary, I see someone I must speak to," she said and quickly made her way toward Joan, who had finished her task and was retreating from the room.

Bess finally caught up with her in the passageway between the great hall and the kitchens.

"Joan! I thought that was you!" she exclaimed, putting on her brightest smile.

If Joan was surprised at the sight of Bess, she did not show it, instead matched Bess' smile with one of her own. "It's fine to see you, Miss, and in such a pretty dress, too."

Bess was taken aback by the pleasantness of her manner, had expected something else entirely, but responded cheerily, "I am heartened to see that you have found such an excellent position, and at such short notice!"

"Aye. I was lucky, Miss," she replied, backing away slightly before adding, "I'm expected back in the kitchens."

"Of course, but first I must ask you something of great importance."

Bess thought she saw Joan's countenance betray a slight anxiousness, and saw her opportunity to increase her discomfort by asking, "Why were you looking through my father's business papers, Joan?"

"I'm sure I don't know what you mean," she answered, looking back toward the kitchens in hope of escape.

Bess moved forward, as if to prevent her flight, and continued, "Alice saw you in his antechamber. That is why you were dismissed. Surely you have not forgotten so soon?"

"I remember now. I was just cleaning up, Miss."

"I am fairly certain that Sir Charles would not condone your 'cleaning up' of his private chamber, just as my father did not. Perhaps I should make him aware of the circumstances surrounding your dismissal?" Bess threatened, expecting to frighten the servant into revealing the motive behind her actions.

She was shocked, therefore, to see Joan give her a look of victorious defiance as she said, "You go right ahead and do that, Miss. Now I really must get back to my chores."

She watched dumbfounded as Joan turned and went back into the kitchens, pausing just long enough to show Bess the small smile that had spread across her face.

The rest of the feast passed without incident. Bess conversed with her friends, ate of the seven-course meal that had been painstakingly prepared, and danced all of the dances but one. When it was almost time for the guests to depart, Sir Charles stood with his daughter Jane on the dais and begged everyone's attention.

"As most of you are aware, my dearest child Jane, who is just turned sixteen, has another cause for rejoicing on this grand day. It is my pleasure to announce that she is officially betrothed to John Coggeshall of Essex."

The crowd clapped its approval.

Sir Charles continued, raising his cup in the air, "Please join with me in congratulating her on a most auspicious match!"

Bess raised her cup with the other guests and drank to Jane's happiness. She could see William through the crowd, who returned her gaze with a sly smile and a wink, as if to say, "I told you so!"

After that, all were free to leave, which Bess and William prepared to do as quickly as possible. As they waited for their carriage to be brought to the front of the house by their groom, Sir Charles surprised them by clapping William on the back, saying, "I know you must be disappointed, my boy. I had always hoped that you and Jane might...well, no need to rub salt in the wound, aye?"

Bess could see William struggle to keep his composure, answering with as serious a face as he could muster, "Very kind of you, Sir."

Sir Charles turned his attention now to Bess. "And when might we hear of your betrothal, young lady?"

Bess could not help but blush, knew Sir Charles did not expect a response when he threw his purple cloak about his shoulders, preparing to take his leave. He fastened his cloak with a lovely silver clasp and put on his jaunty hat before bidding them farewell.

"The matters of a businessman are never completed, as I am sure you know full well. Good day to you both."

They murmured a polite goodbye and watched him gallop away on his fine horse. Bess pulled her cloak around her more tightly in an effort to keep away the cold. The clear day had turned into a cool, crisp evening and she was thankful to be going home. Their groom soon appeared and they climbed into the carriage, thankful for the warmth of their heavy woolen blanket.

William was the first to speak, chiding his sister, "Did I not tell you that some of your friends are becoming betrothed already? Perhaps now you will bend your mind in that direction and act as befits a lady, not a young scoundrel."

Bess was about to take offense when she saw the sparkle in her brother's eye and the look of mischief on his face, knew him to be poking fun at her.

"William Cardwell, I am not about to become betrothed simply to keep up with the rest of my acquaintance. I will marry when it pleases me, not you."

"Well said, little sister. I only hope that father will agree with your sentiment. I have heard him say how impressed he is with Francis Dunkle, and I am certain he is even more impressed with the Dunkle family's wealth. You have met Francis, have you not?"

Bess poked her brother in the ribs with her elbow. "You know full well that I cannot abide Francis! You are a beast to even suggest such a thing," she replied playfully, then stopped and in all earnestness asked, "Father does not truly want me to marry Francis, does he?"

William laughed. "Do not worry, Bess. Father has set his sights a tad higher than the Dunkles."

Bess let out a relieved sigh. Her relief, however, was quickly replaced by anxiousness as to what type of husband her father might have in mind for her. The thought of being no more than a pawn to him and his ambition made her stomach turn.

William continued, "In all seriousness, what were you thinking going into the forest at night to meet that strange man?"

Bess frowned. She had hoped this reckoning would not come, but that was obviously too much to ask for. "He had left a note for Jasmine asking her to meet him that night."

William rolled his eyes. "I knew it was all her fault!"

"Do not be too hasty in blaming Jasmine. She was against my going, but I would not let her venture out alone and forced her to let me accompany her."

"Why did you do such a thing?"

"Because she is my friend. Quite possibly the truest friend I have ever known. I know she is not of our station, Will, but she has a heart of gold, I assure you."

"She is certainly the boldest girl I have ever seen," William acquiesced. "I cannot credit her sense, though, in speaking to a man like that in such a sharp manner!"

"Once you get to know her, you will find that Jasmine is as brave as she is honest."

"How was Mrs. Stopplewick's apple tart, lass?"

"Excellent as always, Papa," Jasmine lied again to her father.

They were at the Black Ox eating a midday meal of lamprey pies. Mr. Bowles had surprised his daughter by inviting her to come with him that afternoon. They had eaten together at the Black Ox in the past, but not many times since her mother's death, and not at all recently.

"What are your plans for today?" he asked.

"I must finish the laundry and then run across the bridge to Skeldergate to deliver Edgar's tunic."

"That's quite a long way," Mr. Bowles commented between mouthfuls. "Why doesn't he fetch it himself?"

"He has much work to do. It seems a wealthy landowner has requested a goodly number of shields to be made."

Mr. Bowles furrowed his brow. "I hope that doesn't bode ill for the future. Did he say who?"

"I don't think he knows," Jasmine answered. "Very secretive business, it seems."

"Hmm," was the only comment from her worried father.

After their lunch, Jasmine went about her chores and managed to be on her way to Skeldergate by late afternoon.

Passing through the marketplace, she caught a glimpse of the traveling troupe of actors performing a Hallowmas play upon a hastily constructed wooden stage. The actors would remain in the city and perform again tomorrow, on All Soul's Day. Jasmine had always fancied that day. She usually found that there was a feeling of happiness in the air; people seemed to be more open and friendly. Of course the fact that the bakers gave away free pastries, called All Soul's rolls, contributed much to her enjoyment.

Edgar the shield-maker lived on the north end of Skeldergate. Jasmine crossed over the Ouse Bridge and soon found her way to his shop. She spotted Edgar in the rear of the wooden building, inspecting a large shield emblazoned with a cross on its surface. Jasmine was doubtful she could even lift such a weighty piece of metalwork, let alone wield a sword in addition. Thankful that she hadn't been born a boy, Jasmine crossed the room, feeling the heat of the shield-maker's fires becoming more oppressive with every step.

Gaining Edgar's attention, she removed the lightweight tunic from her sack and showed him her handiwork. She was certain he would be pleased; she had used the best wool and had spent extra time fashioning the piece. She was disappointed therefore, when he barely acknowledged her, so intent was he upon his business.

"Please lass," he began without looking at her, "You'll find my wife at home next door. She'll pay you whatever you require."

"Yes, sir," Jasmine responded, looking dejected. Hastily putting the tunic back in her sack, she left the shop as quickly as possible.

Edgar had said the house next door, but in which direction had he meant? Jasmine went to her left and knocked on the first door she found. It was opened by a woman holding a child of no more than one year who was crying inconsolably.

"Are you the wife of Edgar?" she asked.

"Can't say that I am," the woman answered good-naturedly. "You'll find her two doors that way," she said, pointing to the right.

"Thank you very much," said Jasmine, relieved that the woman hadn't been angry at her ill-timed interruption. She turned from the door and began retracing her steps. She got as far as the corner of the house when she spotted the under-sheriff, Thomas Wainwright, ducking into a passageway on the other side of the street. She followed him, hoping to overtake him and ask whether or not he had had success in finding the man in black.

He led her onto a narrow path which wound its way through several buildings until they emerged with the river Ouse directly in front of them. He made a sharp turn to the left, and was now facing the same bridge that Jasmine had crossed just a short time ago. When he reached its massive supporting pillars, he went under, veering toward the water's edge.

Jasmine crouched next to the bridge, waiting to see what the under-sheriff could possibly be up to. Pursuing a criminal, perhaps? A clandestine meeting with an informant? In truth, she did feel slightly foolish following him. Why had she not simply called out his name to gain his attention? For some reason she had felt compelled not to do so. Was it something in his manner which made her aware of the secrecy of his actions? Whatever the cause, she was filled with excitement waiting to see what would happen next. She could not be more surprised, however, when she saw who awaited the sheriff. There, perched on the bank of the river, was the man in black!

"It is as I said, Bess. Thomas Wainwright met secretly with the man in black. I saw him with my own eyes," Jasmine argued. She had gone to Cardwell Hall the following morning to tell her friend what she had seen under the Ouse Bridge and to find out if Bess had had any luck in questioning Joan.

"But it is the way you are saying it that gives me pause," Bess replied quickly. "A secret meeting? That sounds entirely too ominous in my opinion. We ourselves asked the sheriff to find and question the man in black and now that he has, you are ready to convict him of every falseness? That seems uncommonly harsh, in truth!"

"Very well. Let us believe the best of Thomas Wainwright. Let us say that he was interrogating the man in black. Why, then, the remoteness of the meeting place? Why did I see them shake hands at the end of the interview? It appeared entirely too conspiratorial to me!"

Bess admitted to herself that the picture did look bleak. "Then we must seek out the sheriff, demand to know what they spoke of."

Jasmine agreed. "And I know just where to look. The actors are performing in the marketplace again today. The scene is ripe for petty thievery, and if Thomas is smart, he will be there rounding up perpetrators."

"Excellent idea! Shall I tell you of my disastrous encounter with Joan on the way?"

Jasmine didn't like the sound of that, but consented nonetheless, and waited until they were walking briskly toward the marketplace before hearing Bess' news of Joan.

"She would tell me nothing, even when I threatened exposure to Sir Charles! She seemed to think it humorous that I would suggest such a thing!" Bess said in disbelief.

Jasmine walked for a moment in silence, pondering the implications of this. "If we cannot find out from Joan what was on that note, we have no hope of ever knowing its contents!"

"We still have Thomas," Bess reminded her. "Perhaps he will tell us what he found out from the man in black and then help us in gaining information from Joan."

Jasmine eyed her friend piteously. Was she naïve in thinking the best of the sheriff, or perhaps blind to his faults for an entirely different reason? Either way, she hoped that Bess would not be overly hurt when they found out the truth.

Bess watched as the minstrels played a jaunty tune, praising King Edward and his Queen, Elizabeth. She and Jasmine had yet to find the sheriff in the marketplace, although they hadn't been looking very hard, so distracted were they with all the lively entertainment surrounding them. They had stopped at a nearby bakery and received their free All Soul's rolls, then watched the end of a play in which God threw Lucifer out of paradise and relegated him to the fiery pit forever. It was quite a dramatic performance and the people had cheered loudly when it came to its conclusion.

Now, as she listened to the music extolling the love shared by King Edward and his Queen, Elizabeth, she was reminded of Thomas, and wished desperately to locate him so that he could explain his actions of yesterday.

"Shall we see if we can find the sheriff?" she asked Jasmine.

"I've been keeping a lookout, but haven't as yet spotted him," she answered. "Perhaps he is near the food vendors' carts."

They were about to begin their search when they heard a voice behind them.

"Enjoying the music, ladies?"

Bess turned, saw that it was Thomas, and blushed deeply. "Very much," she replied. "Who cannot but be moved by such a heartfelt song of love?"

"Indeed. Although I hear that King Edward is hardly the saintly monarch they sing of." He leaned closer to Bess. "They say he bears much love, but not only for his queen."

Bess blushed even more at the scandalous words spoken by the sheriff, but replied evenly, "It is folly to take rumor and innuendo too much to heart, sir. If you can name your source of information, I might be persuaded to believe you."

Thomas smiled, obviously enjoying this exchange. "I have ways of knowing these things; you have only to trust my word."

Jasmine had been listening with piqued interest, now broke into the conversation by asking, "Speaking of your word, sheriff; you had promised to try to find the mysterious man in black that we had told you about. Any luck as yet?"

"Alas, no," the sheriff told her. "I have not been able to locate him."

As he spoke these words, Bess' countenance shifted from elation to dismay, and she found that she could no longer look at his face. How could he lie to them without even blinking an eye? He had seemed full of integrity but moments ago, now he was a man just like any other – as shiftless as the Yorkshire moors.

Jasmine was not surprised by his error of omission, however; had fully expected the answer she had received. "That is passing strange," she said with a purposefully confused look. "I could have sworn I saw you yesterday by the Ouse bridge, speaking with the very same man you deny finding."

The sheriff could not hide his surprise, but carefully regained his composure as he replied, "You must have been mistaken. Now if you'll excuse me, I have many things to do on such a rowdy holiday."

Bess watched as he made his hasty departure. She found that she could not look at Jasmine, so ashamed was she by her own naivety.

"I'm sorry, Bess. Truly I am."

"How could he do such a thing? To stand not an arm's length away, look us in the eyes and lie as he did? It is utterly reprehensible!"

Jasmine was struck by Bess' words. Had she not done the same thing to her father many times?

"And to think he was someone I trusted," Bess continued. "Someone I thought I…" her words died in her throat. She could not betray so much, even to Jasmine.

"Do not fret, Bess. You are not the first to be blinded by a man's good looks and charm. The important thing is that we now know where we stand."

"Yes," Bess replied with a heavy heart. "All alone."

When Bess had told Jasmine that she wished to return home, Jasmine could not blame her friend; in truth, she was depressed as well. She felt as though she had just run into a stone wall and despaired of ever finding out what had really happened that night in the stables or who had murdered the thief.

Now, as the girls returned through the festivities that just moments ago had proven so joyful, neither could find any reason for lightheartedness. They were both hesitant, therefore, when Mrs. Stopplewick came happily bounding in their direction.

"Jasmine, my dear!" she exclaimed, with a gleam in her eyes. "How are you enjoying this fine day?"

"Very well, Mrs. Stopplewick," Jasmine replied. Then remembering her manners, introduced Bess to the jolly woman.

"Pleased to meet you, I'm sure," Mrs. Stopplewick said to Bess, extending her hand.

Bess took it with a forced smile, then noticed the fine clasp that fastened the woman's cloak about her shoulders. "What a beautiful clasp," she remarked. "It must be very dear."

"Aye, that it is. Have you met my Harry?" she asked. When Bess nodded, she continued, "He's the one who gave it to me. Very precious, although it's only brass of course. We're not rich like yourself, dearie. Goodness no!"

Bess' mind went into a whirl. She had seen that clasp before! It was the exact duplicate of the golden clasp she had seen Sir Charles wear when he had visited Cardwell Hall. She quickly remembered that his cloak had been fastened with a different clasp at Jane's birthday feast. She was flooded with a multitude of ideas and asked impatiently, "When did Harry give you the clasp?"

Jasmine was shocked not only by the impertinence of the question, but also the manner in which Bess had asked it.

Mrs. Stopplewick, however, didn't show any sign of offense, merely replied, "Why, I do believe he gave it to me last Thursday. I remember because it was the day before our house was broken into. I was so relieved to have worn it that morn; who knows, if I hadn't, that scoundrel might have stolen it!"

Bess gleamed at Jasmine, who stared at her blankly. "Thank you, Mrs. Stopplewick!" Bess exclaimed. "So nice to have met you!"

She grabbed Jasmine's hand and pulled her along through the crowd, heading for The Shambles.

Jasmine stopped her friend. "What has gotten into you, Bess?" she inquired impatiently.

"We need to speak in private. I have much to tell you!"

When Jasmine still wouldn't budge, Bess explained, "I know who murdered the thief!"

Chapter Nine

Jasmine could hardly contain her excitement, had found it difficult to wait until they arrived at her house to hear what Bess had to say. Now that they were finally sitting on the settle in her front room, Jasmine burst forth, "Tell me, Bess! Who killed the thief?"

"He was murdered by Sir Charles Heatherton!" Bess announced, quite pleased with herself.

"I have heard of him, of course," Jasmine responded. "How on earth did you come to that conclusion? Was it something about Mrs. Stopplewick's clasp?"

"You mean Sir Charles' clasp!"

Jasmine looked bewildered.

"Perhaps it will help if I start from the beginning," Bess suggested.

"Yes, please do!"

"A little while ago Sir Charles visited Cardwell Hall and I happened to meet him coming out of my father's antechamber. He was wearing his purple cloak, which was fastened with an intricately carved golden clasp. I remember thinking it was quite lovely at the time. You will recall that I went to Jane Heatherton's birthday feast yesterday?"

Jasmine nodded impatiently.

"When Will and I were leaving, Sir Charles came out and spoke to us before riding off on his horse. He was wearing the same purple cloak, but it was fastened with a different clasp! When I saw Mrs. Stopplewick wearing the original gold clasp, I knew that I had seen it before, and when she told me that it had been given to her by Harry the day after the murder in the stables...well, it is obvious is it not?"

Jasmine was quick to put the pieces of the puzzle together. "Harry lied to us about not finding anything else in the stables. There had obviously been a struggle that night and the thief probably grabbed at Sir Charles as he was being stabbed and pulled the clasp off the cloak. Harry found the clasp, along with the money, and made a present of it to his mother!"

"Exactly."

"So it was Sir Charles who ransacked Harry's house, hoping to find his clasp."

Bess disagreed. "It is highly unlikely that a man of Sir Charles' stature would break into the Stopplewick's house himself. He most certainly would have sent someone else to do it; someone who was already in his confidence. Could the man in black be working for Sir Charles?"

"That does seem to fit. He ransacked Harry's house and, finding nothing, accosted Harry, trying to find out if he had taken the clasp from the stables."

"This also explains how Joan found another post so soon after Alice dismissed her," Bess remarked, "and why she found the threat to inform Sir Charles so amusing!"

Jasmine could hardly believe they had solved the mystery just as they had given up all hope, and marveled that it had all been due to a chance meeting in the crowded marketplace of York.

"Jasmine?" Bess interrupted her thoughts. "Does this mean that since the sheriff is in collusion with the man in black, he is also involved in Sir Charles' plot?"

Jasmine hated to admit it, but it did sound likely. "Do you remember his quickness to attribute the thief's murder to foul play among fellow criminals? He certainly had no intention of looking into the matter. I'm afraid it does look bad for Thomas Wainwright."

Bess was crushed. That Thomas had lied to them was bad enough; now to find out that he might have been involved in a murderous plot was too much to take. "I simply will not believe it," she said with as much conviction as she could muster. "I refuse to think the worst of him without any tangible evidence."

Jasmine had to admire the loyalty of her friend, however misplaced it might be. "Very well then. Let us go to Thomas Wainwright, tell him what we know and see if he will do anything about it."

Bess was shocked at this idea. "What if he tells Sir Charles of our suspicions? We might be placing ourselves in serious danger!"

"Then we decide not to trust the sheriff, instead go to one of the higher ranking sheriffs and tell him the whole story."

Bess pondered the two options and came to her conclusion. Since she could never truly believe Thomas capable of doing anything that would put them in danger, her choice was clear. "We must tell Thomas everything."

Jasmine had not been surprised by Bess' decision to tell all they knew to the sheriff; in truth, she was glad. If Thomas was involved, his actions after hearing their story would remove all doubt and they could then go to another sheriff, exposing not only Sir Charles, but Thomas as well.

They had little difficulty in finding him. Returning to the marketplace, they saw that a fight had broken out among the revelers, and the sheriff was even now trying to sort out the melee.

Bess watched as Thomas spoke calmly, yet authoritatively, inducing the participants in the quarrel to cease their rowdy behavior and retreat from the area. He then disbursed the on-lookers, even managing to elicit laughter by a well-timed pun. She felt certain her choice to trust him would not be in vain.

Since they had not left with the rest of the crowd, they soon found themselves face to face with Thomas, who did not look overly pleased to see them there.

"Sheriff..." Jasmine began, uncertain of how to proceed. Seeing his look of impatience at her hesitation, she decided that the direct approach would be best. "Do you remember the thief who stole Bess' pouch who was murdered in the blacksmith's stables?" When she saw him give her a quick nod, she continued, "Bess and I know who killed him."

He caught them off-guard with his laughter. "You do, eh? Well, I suppose we had better move to a more private location, do you not think? We would not want to be overheard, would we?"

Bess and Jasmine didn't know what to make of his reaction; it certainly wasn't what they had been hoping for, or expecting. They followed him to a secluded alleyway between two shop fronts and when he folded his arms and leaned against the stone wall, Jasmine could tell that he was now ready to hear their tale. She told him about Harry taking the money and clasp from the stables. She told him about Joan and the note, and that Joan was now in the service of Sir Charles. She told him that it was Sir Charles' clasp that Harry had found, which his mother now wore on her cloak. She told him everything she could think of to make him believe in Sir Charles' guilt.

Bess watched Thomas closely as Jasmine related what they had discovered. His face showed neither shock nor disbelief; his countenance was as impassive as stone, and just as cold. She felt a sickness in the pit of her stomach. Were they making a huge mistake?

When Jasmine had finished speaking, Thomas took a deep breath, looked at Bess, then back at

Jasmine before saying, "Where are Harry and Mrs. Stopplewick now?"

Bess answered, "We do not know."

"Find them as quickly as possible, take them to their house and bolt the door behind you."

He said no more, obviously expecting them to do his bidding immediately. Jasmine needed more information, however, and asked, "And what will you be doing?"

Thomas showed his impatience by grabbing Jasmine by the shoulders, turning her around and giving her a little push, shouting, "Hurry! There is no time to lose!"

Both girls ran as fast as they could down the alleyway and into the marketplace, Bess stopping only for a moment to look back, but Thomas was nowhere to be seen. They charged through the streets, searching for Harry and his mother. Seeing his friend Tom, Jasmine asked if he knew Harry's whereabouts.

"Aye. He was here a second ago, then took off. Said he needed to meet his mother in the Shambles.

Something about helping her carry home some heavy meat."

She and Bess raced through the streets to Jasmine's home, knowing Mrs. Stopplewick always bought her meat from her father. They arrived just in time to see Mr. Bowles handing Mrs. Stopplewick a fine slab of mutton. Both girls saw immediately that she was wearing her cloak with the golden clasp proudly displayed. Rushing toward them, Jasmine grabbed Harry and told him they must get his mother back to their house immediately.

"Whatever are you talking about, Jasmine?" he asked, looking perplexed.

"There is no time to explain. You do trust me, do you not?" When Harry nodded wordlessly, she exclaimed, "Then hurry! We must get to your home as soon as possible!"

Jasmine was thankful when Harry took the meat from his mother, saying, "Let me carry this home for you. Jasmine and Bess are coming with us. They're both wanting a cup of your Tansy tea."

Mrs. Stopplewick was obviously pleased, led the way to her home with as much pride as a mother hen. Jasmine paused only to speak to her father.

"Is anything amiss, lass?" he inquired.

"No, Papa. I will tell you all when I return, truly." She kissed her father on the cheek and hurried to rejoin the others.

Jasmine was glad the Stopplewick home was only a short distance around the corner from the Shambles, although it had crossed her mind that perhaps they should have sought refuge in her home instead. But she had chosen to obey Thomas' instructions, could now only hope that she had made the correct decision.

Once inside, Jasmine bolted the door, causing Mrs. Stopplewick to look perplexed as she said, "There's no need to bolt the door," then seeing their worried faces asked, "is there?"

Jasmine looked at Harry. "Isn't there something you would like to tell your mother?"

Harry looked uncomfortable. "I don't know what you mean."

"Something about the clasp on her cloak, perhaps?" Bess suggested.

"You know?" he asked with a mixture of fear and disbelief.

Jasmine nodded her head. "We even know who killed the thief that night in the stables, and why your home was ransacked two days later."

Mrs. Stopplewick surprised them by calmly saying, "I think we had all better sit down at the table. I'll fetch us some tea; then one of you can start from the beginning and tell me all about it."

They wordlessly did as she bade and waited at the table until she had brought them all a steaming hot cup of Tansy tea.

"Jasmine, my dear, would you like to tell me your story?" Mrs. Stopplewick asked.

Jasmine cleared her throat and began telling her all about the events leading up to the episode in the blacksmith's stables, and also Harry's involvement in them. She then related how she and Bess had endeavored to solve the mystery behind the murder of the thief, and how they eventually had. She even told her about their secret meeting with the man in black in the forest on Hallowmas.

Once she was finished, and a hush had overtaken the room, Mrs. Stopplewick looked at her son, then silently crossed the room and opened up her sewing box. Retrieving the necessary instrument, she then grabbed her cloak and began hastily removing the clasp. Once she was finished, she looked again at Harry and said, "I will not have anything in this house that was not properly earned by good, honest work. Is that clear?"

"Yes, Mama," Harry sheepishly replied, unable to look at his mother as he spoke.

Bess had as yet been a silent witness to these proceedings, now wished she could say something to ease the tension in the room. Her thoughts were interrupted, however, by a loud banging on the door which caused everyone to jump to their feet.

"Maybe it is Thomas," Bess hoped aloud.

Jasmine went and stood a few feet from the door. "Who's there?"

Her question was answered by more banging and then a voice yelling, "Let me in!"

"That is not Thomas' voice!" Bess exclaimed.

They all stood as if frozen, not knowing what they should do. The banging suddenly ceased.

"Maybe he's giving up," Harry wished aloud.

Jasmine highly doubted that, wondered if he was getting ready to smash through the door, when she spotted the window. "The shutters!" she exclaimed. "They are not bolted!" She ran to the window, but before she could reach the latch the shutters flew open. Her heart almost stopped beating when she saw the face of the man in black!

She heard Bess scream, turned and ran to her friend's side. Mrs. Stopplewick had fled to the corner of the room with Harry, and they now attempted to seek refuge in her bedchamber. The man in black was too quick, however, had already climbed through the window and rushed to the bedchamber door before they could reach it.

He looked down at Mrs. Stopplewick's hands, which were still holding the clasp and said, "I'll take that, if you please."

She thrust the clasp at him, saying, "Good riddance! Now please leave my home!"

"I am afraid I cannot do that. Well, not yet," he replied, looking at Jasmine and Bess.

Bess squeezed Jasmine's hand, hoping her friend would understand her wordless apology. This was all her fault! She had trusted Thomas Wainwright, was now paying the price for her foolishness. They had walked right into his trap!

Before anyone else could move, they heard a noise at the door; someone was trying the latch.

Bess whispered, "It is Thomas."

The man in black said to Jasmine, "Ask who it is."

Not wanting to cooperate with him, she remained silent.

"Need I remind you that you are in imminent danger?" He kept his voice low, but the look in his eyes made Jasmine understand his meaning all too clearly. "Now ask who it is!"

This time she went to the door and yelled, "Who's there?"

She heard no response, only a giant thud as if something large and heavy was being thrust into the door. Jasmine backed away slowly, keeping her eyes on the latch as it began to break away from the door.

A few seconds later, the door was flung open, revealing not Thomas, but Sir Charles!

He seemed surprised to see Jasmine, but his jaw dropped at sight of Bess.

Jasmine went to her friend, who had retreated behind the table, and was joined by Harry and his mother. She then noticed that the man in black had disappeared.

Sir Charles walked toward them until he reached the table.

Bess looked at him with revulsion and asked, "How could you?"

"How could I what? Betray your father? Murder a no-good thief? The answer is simple - politics, my dear, politics."

"What do you mean?"

"King Edward has no love for York, although he was brought up on its moors. No, he blames us northerners for backing old King Henry and Margaret, could never forgive our Lancastrian tendencies. The great merchant families of the north are facing an uphill battle as long as King Edward is on the throne, I assure you."

"You want to depose Edward?" Jasmine asked incredulously.

"Now you are getting the picture. Henry and Margaret's son will rule someday, and he will owe the people of York, particularly me, a great debt," Sir Charles said with a gleam in his eye.

"But what has this to do with my father?" Bess asked. "What information did Joan sneak out of his antechamber for you?"

"If I told you that, young lady, I would have to kill you. And we certainly would not want that, would we?"

Bess looked at him coldly.

"Now if you will hand over the clasp," Sir Charles asked Harry.

"Is this what you are looking for?"

Jasmine and Bess turned toward the bedchamber door as the man in black emerged holding the golden clasp.

"You!" Sir Charles exclaimed, removing a dagger from his belt.

"That is not necessary, I can assure you," he said, flipping the clasp in the air and catching it effortlessly. "You have as much chance of piercing me with that thing as I have of sprouting wings."

Sir Charles knew he was right and looked about him wildly. He grabbed Jasmine by the hair and dragged her out from behind the table. "Aye, but I can pierce her if you do not hand it over!"

Bess gave a shriek, looked to see what the man in black would do now. His face had grown ashen, as though he had not expected such a turn of events.

"You may have it then," he said, throwing the clasp at Sir Charles' feet.

Sir Charles picked it up with a look of triumph. Keeping hold of Jasmine, the dagger aimed at her heart, he backed toward the door, all the while eyeing the man in black. He reached the threshold and shoved Jasmine to the floor, hoping to make his getaway. With a victorious laugh he turned to escape, only to find the sheriff and his men awaiting him.

"Thomas!" Bess exclaimed with a relief beyond anything she had felt before. She immediately ran to Jasmine, who was being helped up by the man in black.

"Thank you, sir," Jasmine said to him shyly, then hugged Bess in joy and exhaustion.

"Am I glad to see you!" the man in black said to Thomas, who had already instructed his men to take Sir Charles to the gaol.

"Seems we were just in time," he replied, then looked softly at Bess and Jasmine. "You are not hurt?"

They both shook their heads and received hugs from Mrs. Stopplewick and Harry.

"Let me get you both a cup of hot tea," Mrs. Stopplewick said to the men, as though they had just arrived for a social call.

"Thank you, but no," Thomas said decisively. "We still have much work to do."

"Sheriff?" Bess said.

"You called me Thomas but moments before. Must we go back to such formality so soon?"

Bess blushed. "Thomas," she said with deliberate slowness. "What will happen to Sir Charles?"

"He will be sent to London to await trial and sentencing."

"Sentencing? You are certain he will be found guilty?" Jasmine asked.

"King Edward has little patience for traitors," the man in black responded.

"But what is your proof of treason? The golden clasp proves that he murdered the thief. That is all."

"You are forgetting Joan," Thomas reminded her. "I have her in custody. She was more than willing to reveal all in order to save her own skin."

"She told you the contents of the note?" Bess excitedly asked.

Thomas nodded. "You know that the quarterly profits for the Wool Merchants Guild are due to the King, and that your father is in charge of its transport to London?"

"Yes, of course."

"Were you also aware that the date and route of the transport were known only to your father and the Guild's treasurer to ensure its safekeeping?"

"I had no idea."

"The note that Joan placed inside your pouch contained this information. Sir Charles was planning to steal the Wool Merchants Guild's shipment in order to fund a Lancastrian rebellion, hoping to put King Henry's son on the throne."

"Yes, he told us of his political aims," Jasmine remarked. "What I don't understand is why they decided to put the note in Bess' pouch in the first place. I can see why it would be difficult for Joan and Sir Charles to be seen together, but why did Joan not simply tell the thief the secret information and let him relate it to Sir Charles?"

"It was a matter of trust. The thief couldn't read or write, so Sir Charles was certain that only he knew the details of the shipment," Thomas explained.

Bess added, "And she only gained the information the afternoon before the theft, when she was caught rummaging through my father's antechamber. She must have made plans with the thief earlier, telling him the information would be on a note inside my pouch and to go to the blacksmith's stables to deliver it in return for five pounds."

"Was he murdered because he was trying to garner more money, or because Sir Charles didn't want anyone else knowing he was involved?" Jasmine pondered.

"That," the man in black replied, "only Sir Charles can answer. Now if you'll excuse me, I must make ready for London." He smiled in farewell and left the Stopplewick home.

Jasmine was still reeling from the turn of events. She had mistaken the man in black for a villain and had treated him with contempt. In truth, he had brought most of it upon himself with his secrecy and unexplainable actions. Still, she felt as though she owed him an apology, and now it was too late.

"I, too, must be off," Thomas told them. "Your father can be found at the Merchant Adventurer's Hall, can he not?" he asked Bess, who nodded. "He needs to be told of this plot at once so he may change the route of the shipment. Sir Charles most certainly had a plan already in motion that might still be carried out, even without him."

"I had not thought of that, in truth," Bess replied.

"It is a good thing that I am the sheriff then, is it not?"

Bess laughed. "A very good thing."

Thomas said his farewells to Harry and his mother, then told Jasmine and Bess to go home. "You need your rest after such an eventful day," he said, then added as he made his way out the door, "and I don't want you two involved in any more intrigue, is that understood?"

They replied, "Yes, sir!" in unison, believing it would be a promise easily kept.

Chapter Ten

Jasmine reached her home just as her father was closing up shop. He looked at her sadly, and Jasmine felt as though she was looking at a stranger. She wasn't surprised; hadn't they been living as strangers lately?

"I'll be up in a moment, lass," he told her.

She went upstairs and began preparing their supper, her mind in a whirl trying to think of the right words to say to her father. How could she tell him that she had been lying to him for weeks? That she had lied first about playing football, then about her secret activities. She knew he would be angry, but what tore her apart was that she also knew he would be hurt.

"Jasmine?" she heard coming from the outer room. "Could you come here, please?"

She gave the pot one last stir, then went to confront her father. She found him sitting on the settle, his head in his hands.

"Yes, Papa?"

"Sit beside me, Jasmine. I need to talk to you."

He rarely spoke to her in such earnestness, and his tone made Jasmine all the more worried. She sat next to him and prepared for the worst.

"I haven't seen much of you these past few days. Have you been spending time with the Cardwell girl?"

"Yes. I want to tell you…"

Mr. Bowles raised his hand to stop her speech. "First let me say a few words, lass. I know it's been a rough couple of weeks for you; it has been for me as well. The anniversary of your mother's death hit me hard, in truth, and I'm sure you felt the same. But we can't go on shutting each other out. I need to be included in your life, and need to include you more in mine. It's not fair to expect you to shoulder your grief alone; we should be able to comfort each other. I know I've been unable to do that, and I want to say I'm sorry."

Jasmine was dumbfounded. She had assumed her father was angry with her, had certainly not expected what she had just heard. "I'm sorry too, Papa."

Before she could say any more, he put his heavy arms around her and gave her a big hug. Jasmine felt the tears welling up inside her and before she could control her emotions, she began to sob. She cried at the words her father had just spoken, then cried harder thinking of the words she had yet to speak.

"Papa," she said, pulling away from him. "There is much I have to tell you."

Her father rubbed his eyes and looked at her expectantly, as if he knew what was to come.

"I'm ashamed to say that I've been lying to you. I lied to you about playing football. I lied to you when I told you I went to the Stopplewick's for apple tarts on Hallowmas. I cannot even remember what other lies I have told you, but I want to apologize for each and every one of them. I promise I will not betray your trust again."

Mr. Bowles looked upon his daughter with a mixture of disappointment and love. "I'm hurt by your words, I'll not deny that. But I do appreciate them. Why don't we turn over a new leaf, so to speak, eh? No more lying, no more ignoring our feelings. What do you say to that?"

Jasmine was amazed by her father's kindness, gave him a big kiss of gratitude.

"Now why don't you tell me what's been going on in your life?" he asked.

"Gladly, Papa," she replied, and began to tell him about her friendship with Bess, the mystery behind the theft of her pouch, and how they had solved the murder of the thief. When she was finished, she saw the look of admiration and pride in her father's eyes and knew that everything was going to be fine.

Bess returned to Cardwell Hall, found Alice alone in the solar.

"Have my father and William returned yet?" she asked her step-mother.

"No," Alice responded, looking up from her needlework.

Bess took a seat on the settle opposite and folded her hands in her lap. "I have something I wish to say to you."

"By all means," Alice replied, "as long as you are not planning on accusing me of stealing your pouch again. I am assuming you no longer suspect me of... what was it? Trying to deliver secret information?"

Bess hung her head low. She was ashamed of herself. She had been so wrong about so many things, could only hope to somehow make it right. "I am truly sorry, Alice. I should not have blamed you for the theft of my pouch. I was utterly wrong and I hope you can forgive me."

Alice went back to her needlework and said, "Yes, I can forgive you."

Bess knew better than to expect a more heartfelt response, knew this was but the first step in a lengthy process of mending fences with her step-mother. She rose and exited the solar, finding William crossing the great hall anxiously.

"Elizabeth Cardwell!" he exclaimed.

Bess was taken aback. "What is it, Will?"

"I have just returned from the Guild Hall. The sheriff told us all about the plot to steal the Guild's profits. Father is there even now trying to make other plans for their shipment to London. I cannot believe Sir Charles would invent such a scheme, not to mention kill a man!"

"It is shocking, to be sure," Bess replied.

"You are not hurt," he asked, his disbelief being replaced by concern.

"Not physically. But I am emotionally spent, I assure you. Once we knew it was Sir Charles who had killed the thief, we did not know who to turn to, did not know who to trust."

"You could have trusted me, little sister."

"I know, Will, but it all happened so fast. You were at the Guild Hall with father, and we needed to do something right away."

Bess saw that William looked depressed, as if something else was pressing on his mind. She asked, "Is anything else amiss?"

William took a deep breath, ran his hand over his chin, then said, "I suppose I may as well tell you."

Bess cringed at these words; she needed no more surprises today.

"Father is sending me to Middleham after the Christmas festivities."

Bess knew this was what her father had wished for William; an education at Middleham ensured a life of influence in the highest circles. Her father's plan had always included being rich and powerful enough to give his son a place at King Edward's court.

"But surely that is nothing to be sad about! It is an honor to be accepted at Middleham, will assure you a place at court once you are finished."

"I have no desire for the life of a courtier! In truth, the very thought makes me ill! What shall I do, Bess?"

"Have you told father how you feel?"

"More times than I can count. It seems my opinion is of no consequence." William looked at his sister with affection. "Listen to me," he said, "rambling on about my problems, when you have just put a murderer behind bars! I am very proud of you, dearest."

"Thank you, Will. That means a great deal to me. And do not lose hope. We do have until Christmas to change father's mind!"

Bess was in her bedchamber, finishing the tale of the valiant King Arthur. It seemed a lifetime ago since she had last opened her book. She had not known Jasmine then; she had not known Thomas, either. She thought of his kind green eyes, and thanked God she had been proven justified in trusting him. What was amazing to her, though, was that the man in black had turned out to be a friend instead of a foe. But hadn't she and Jasmine started out as enemies at first? The remembrance was almost laughable now. She had been so unhappy before meeting Jasmine, was ready to lash out at anyone who stepped in her path. Thankfully Jasmine had forgiven her; where would she be now if she hadn't?

Bess was startled back into the present by a loud knock on her door.

"Come in," she called, hoping the interruption would be a short one.

The door opened and Sir James Cardwell came in cautiously, as if each step needed assurance. Bess rose from the window seat at sight of her father. She could not remember when he had last been inside her bedchamber. Surely not in these past three years.

He stopped in the middle of the room, and she stood as if frozen. She knew he had heard all about her exploits as Will had. As her father, would he be angry with her for risking so much to find out that Sir Charles was behind the theft of her pouch? Or would he, as the powerful merchant, be grateful that she had saved the money for the King? Unsure of his reaction, she hid her hands in the long sleeves of her gown and waited.

"Princess," he uttered softly, holding his arms out to her.

She could hardly believe her eyes! She flung herself into his arms and they hugged each other as they hadn't for a long, long time.

Then her father backed up a step and looked at her sternly. "If you ever put yourself in harm's way for me again, young lady, you will quickly find yourself behind the thick walls of the nearest nunnery! Is that clear?"

"Yes, Father," she replied with a smirk, knowing him to be jesting.

"Seriously, Bess, you could have been in danger. Sir Charles would have stopped at nothing to see his plans come to fruition!"

"I am sorry. At first, looking into the mystery seemed like a harmless way to pass the hours. Jasmine and I had little hope of finding out why the thief was killed; we simply enjoyed spending time together. Honestly, no one was more surprised than I to actually reveal Sir Charles as the culprit!"

She saw her father's face cloud over, as if still feeling the shock and anger at his friend's betrayal. He quickly regained his composure, however, and said, "You must thank your friend Jasmine for me as well. You both saved our family from ruin, for if something had befallen that shipment to London, I would have been held personally responsible."

"Yes, Father."

His face softened as he took her arm and led her to the window seat. "Sit down, Bess. I do have something else to say to you."

She did as he bade, pondering the content of his next words.

He took her hand. "I know this has not been a happy place for you since I married Alice."

Bess looked at him with surprise.

"Believe it or not, I am not blind, nor am I uncaring of your feelings. I simply assumed that time would heal our household, and put all my energy into building our family's prospects instead of worrying about your relationship with your step-mother. I know it may have appeared as though I had given no thought to you or your troubles, but that is not so. I love you very much and want to see you happy."

"I love you too, Father," Bess replied, amazed at his speech. She couldn't remember the last time they had spoken those words. Before the moment passed, however, she took a chance and asked her father the one question she most needed him to answer.

"Do you not miss Mother anymore? Do you not still love her?"

Sir James put his arms around his daughter. "Of course I miss your mother, dearest. Not a day passes when I do not think of her. She will always have my heart." He looked his daughter in the eyes. "You are growing up so fast. Did you know that you resemble your mother in every way?"

Bess' surprise showed on her face as she shook her head.

"Every day you remind me more of her. It is sometimes painful for me to see."

"I did not know, truly," Bess said, comprehending her father's feelings for the first time. "But I am glad you told me." She looked down at her hands, felt the tears begin to sting her eyes. "I do wish things could be different, I wish..."

"I know, sweetheart," her father replied as he hugged her tightly.

After several moments, Bess was able to look at her father and smile. Smiling back, he squeezed her hand, then stood and made his way toward the door. As he pulled the latch, he turned and said nonchalantly, "Oh yes, I almost forgot. We are leaving for the Manor in two days. You might want to instruct Maude to make ready your things."

Bess stared blankly as the door closed behind him. The Manor! She could not believe that with one little sentence, her father had turned her happiness to sadness. She was not ready to leave York! How she would miss Jasmine! She thought of the activities which awaited her back in the countryside. All the Christmas revelries she normally took such pleasure in now seemed bleak without her friend. It also occurred to her that she might not see Thomas again for a very long time. Had it been her imagination, or had there been a spark of something between them? If she left now, he might forget her.

She plopped upon her bed, clutched a velvet pillow and stared up at her purple canopy, the tale of King Arthur forgotten again.

Jasmine rounded the corner just as the clouds began to pour tiny droplets onto her head. She pulled up the hood of her mantle and continued down the street toward the gaol. If she was lucky, she would arrive in time to see Sir Charles being escorted out of York.

As she approached the gaol, however, she felt a knot in her stomach, knew the real reason for her being here was to see the man in black. She simply could not let him leave for London without discovering how he was involved in the theft of Bess' pouch.

Why had he been following Bess in the marketplace that day? How had he known that Harry was in the blacksmith's stables that night? She had many questions and could only hope that he would provide at least some of the answers.

She could see through the rain that a small caravan was being put into place in front of the gaol. She saw from the number of horses that the city of York was taking no chances when it came to getting Sir Charles to London.

She stopped a safe distance away from the activity and looked about her. There was no sign of Sir Charles; he must still be inside. A couple of the sheriffs were standing in front of the building talking, and curious onlookers like herself were milling about. She did not see Thomas, however, nor did she see the man in black. Could they be inside, perhaps?

She decided to cross the street in order to get a better view of the gaol doorway and, in doing so, provide them with a better glimpse of her. She knew she did not have the courage to confront the man in black herself; her only hope lay in the possibility that he would see her and decide to approach her himself. She knew the likeliness of such a scenario occurring was slim, but she felt she had to try, nonetheless.

As she turned to cross the street, she heard horses' hooves behind her and pulled up suddenly, letting the hooded rider continue toward his destination. He stopped at the back of the caravan and almost jumped from his horse, so intent was he on entering the gaol. Jasmine watched as he approached the doorway, ignoring the men conversing in front of him. Then, to her great surprise, he turned and looked directly at her. She caught her breath as she saw that it was the man in black's grey eyes that were staring into her own!

He slowly began walking toward her and she could not tell if he was pleased to see her or not, so impassive was his expression. She was suddenly indignant. After what they had been through together yesterday, the least he could do was show some emotion! A smile, perhaps? By the time he reached her, she had made up her mind that he was the most aggravating man she had ever met.

"Good day, Miss," he said. "I hope you have recovered from the events of yesterday?"

"I have indeed," she replied evenly. "I didn't get a chance to thank you for intervening when you did. Who knows what Sir Charles might have had in mind? You obviously knew the man, did you not?"

"Our paths had crossed before, I am sorry to say."

"And you are on close terms with Thomas Wainwright, I believe," she persisted.

"I met him just recently, but he seems a fine sort," the man in black replied good-naturedly. Before Jasmine could fire another question, he continued, "I am glad to have bumped into you this morn. I wanted to thank you for finding the proof of Sir Charles' guilt, even when I could not."

Jasmine was shocked by his words of gratitude, could only reply by asking the obvious. "Who are you?"

He threw back his hood, letting the rain fall on his black hair, and leaned forward as if whispering a secret. "I can count on your discretion, can I not?" When Jasmine nodded mutely, he said, "My name is Luke. I am the King's Man."

Jasmine did not wish to appear ignorant, but her overwhelming curiosity won out and she asked, "What does that mean?"

"It means that I do the King's bidding."

"And what did he bid you to do here in York?"

"King Edward has long held the suspicion that Henry's queen, Marguerite, had an agent working inside the Wool Merchant's Guild here in York. He sent me to find out who it was. At first, my inclination told me to suspect Sir James Cardwell. He is father to your friend, is he not?"

"Yes, he is Bess' father."

"After observing his household, however, I soon realized that one of his maids was not to be trusted. I overheard her making plans with the man who stole Bess' pouch. His name was Charlie, by the way, poor sod. So it seems Joan had two Charles' in her life."

"Two too many, if you ask me!" Jasmine interjected.

"Quite true," Luke replied with a grin.

"So you were following Bess in the marketplace hoping to find the thief and apprehend him before he could steal…"

Luke shook his head and interrupted, "No, lass. I wanted him to steal the pouch."

"But if Bess had been hurt…" Jasmine began, looking confused.

"I know. I could only hope that she would not be. But I had to let the thief meet his contact that night. I needed to find out who he was. Unfortunately, your friend Harry got in the way. He scared Sir Charles into leaving in a hurry by the back way and I had no opportunity to see his face."

"So you threatened Harry, wanting to know if he had seen who the contact was?"

"Is that what he told you?" Luke replied with a feigned look of shock. "I did not threaten him. I simply encouraged him to tell me the truth!"

Jasmine saw movement in front of the gaol. Sir Charles was being helped onto a horse. Luke noticed, too.

"Did you break into Harry's house, then?" she asked before he could turn from her.

"My dear young lady," he replied with a spark of mischief. "Some things in life should remain a mystery!"

They looked at each other and grinned. Jasmine regarded his face as if seeing him for the first time. The strong features that once seemed so ominous, now appeared striking and bold. He was younger than she had assumed, could not be more than twenty-seven or twenty-eight.

He looked suddenly serious. "There is something else..."

He was interrupted by one of the sheriffs calling his name. Instead of finishing his sentence, he covered his head again and winked at Jasmine, saying, "Perhaps our paths shall cross again one day."

Jasmine stood motionless as he turned and rejoined the others. She saw him mount his horse and lead the caravan down the street, not once looking back.

Before Jasmine could ponder his words, she felt a tap on her shoulder. Turning around, she saw Harry with an amused look on his face.

"What were you two talking about?" he asked.

"You," Jasmine replied, irked at her friend's timing. "What are you doing here?"

"I came to see Sir Charles being taken out of York, just like you. Unless there was another reason for your coming?" he teased.

She ignored his question. "I hope you realize how lucky you are to still be in one piece? You could have gotten your dear mother hurt as well!"

Harry looked downcast and lowered his head. "Aye, I know. I have already told my mother how sorry I am. In truth, I think she's sick of hearing it so often! But I do want to apologize to you too, Jasmine, for getting you mixed up in this whole mess in the first place. And I want you to know that I'm done with stealing. I swear!"

Far from being touched by his penitance, she asked strictly, "And lying?"

"Aye. And lying, too," he answered, glad she could not see that he had just crossed his fingers behind his back.

Jasmine had been home for several hours since her encounter that morning with Luke. She had many things to do, the work of the day before having been ignored for obvious reasons. She found it difficult to concentrate, however, and opened the shutters in order to gaze out onto the street below. This simple act made her think of Cardwell Hall, with its windows made of glass. Jasmine doubted she and her father would ever be able to afford to put glass in their windows; that was strictly for the wealthy. She allowed herself one more look before closing the shutters against the cold.

"Jasmine!" she heard someone calling from below. She looked out and saw that it was Bess. She ran down the stairs and opened the door to let her friend inside.

"Bess, I'm glad to see you! I have something interesting to tell you!"

Instead of looking excited however, Bess looked miserable. Jasmine led her up the stairs and when the two girls had sat down on the settle, asked, "Whatever is the matter?"

"We are leaving York first thing tomorrow morning!" she exclaimed.

"So soon?"

Bess nodded. "To think that only one week ago I would have been thrilled to be going back to the Manor. How things do change!"

Jasmine knew this day would come, knew Bess could not stay in York forever, but was still surprised nonetheless. "I am going to miss you," she stated simply.

Bess hugged her friend. "I will miss you, too!"

"Wait here a moment," Jasmine told her, and ran into her bedchamber.

Bess did as she bade, then saw Jasmine emerge holding a lovely pink pouch in her hands.

"I made this for you, to replace the one that was stolen." Jasmine held it out to Bess, who rose from the settle, took the silken pouch in her hands and marveled at its perfection. It was beautifully embroidered with blue and yellow flowers and even had a 'B' inscribed on the front. "I know it should have been an 'E' for Elizabeth," Jasmine continued, "but I will always think of you as Bess."

Bess wiped the tears from her eyes, found she could not speak, instead gave Jasmine another hug.

"You do like it?" Jasmine asked.

"Oh yes! It is truly beautiful. I will cherish it always!" She held the pouch gently as she sat again on the settle, saying, "You said you had something interesting to tell me?"

Jasmine told her about her morning encounter with the man in black, informing her that his name is Luke, and that he works for King Edward.

"He works for the King?" Bess repeated, stunned by this information.

"He said that he is the King's Man."

"Ooh," Bess

"You know what that means?"

"Yes, of course. But he should not have told you; the identity of one who works for the King should be kept strictly confidential."

Jasmine blushed in shame. "He did ask me to keep it a secret, but I had to tell you!"

"I am glad you did, although I would have understood if you had not." Bess rose again, as if unsure of what she should do.

Jasmine rose, too, and saw a spark of remembrance cross her friend's face.

"Oh, I almost forgot," Bess said as she untied her pouch from her belt. "Hold out your hands," she instructed Jasmine.

Jasmine did as she bade and was shocked as Bess poured the contents of the pouch into her palms. "What is this?"

"The five pounds," Bess answered, looking pleased.

"Why are you giving it to me?"

"It is not mine."

"But it is not mine, either."

"I suppose it truly belongs to Sir Charles, but since he will have no need of it where his is going, I am giving it to you," Bess told her matter-of-factly.

"I don't think this is right," Jasmine said haltingly, secretly hoping she would be able to keep the money.

"I have talked to my father about it and he is in full agreement, even told me to express his thanks to you for saving the Guild's profits."

"I don't know what to say."

"Then say nothing, but do not forget me." Bess gave Jasmine another quick hug, then said with forced cheerfulness, "I must go now. I need to help prepare for the move to the Manor. Poor Maude is frantic, trying to pack for both my stepmother and for me."

"Of course," Jasmine replied as she laid the five pounds on the table. She led Bess down the stairs, knowing she should say something in farewell, but found that the words would not come. Instead she mutely opened the door.

"I shall write you," Bess said through watery eyes.

Jasmine nodded, wiped her own eyes and said, "And I will be praying that you have a safe journey. And look forward to your letters!"

Bess took Jasmine's hand. "Goodbye, dear friend!" Not waiting for Jasmine's response, she turned and ran down the street.

Jasmine was about to close the door, when her father came to her side.

"Don't fret, lass. You'll see your friend again soon."

"How do you know, Papa?"

"I just know," he said with a wink and a smile, giving his daughter a great big hug.

Jasmine felt safe and secure, and believed her father's words. She went back upstairs, sat again on the window seat and opened the shutters. She looked down onto the hustle and bustle of The Shambles, heard her father's hearty laugh as he joked with a customer, and felt a peace she had not known since her mother's death. She would see Bess again, and they would be friends for a long, long time. She knew this and she thanked God for it.

ABOUT THE AUTHOR

Dianne LeMay is a mixed-media artist and writer. She lives in the beautiful wine country of Oregon with her husband and two daughters.

Visit her website at www.diannelemaystudio.com